BEGOTTEN SON: PART ONE
THE PLAN OF THE ITALIAN MERCHANT

DANNY D

authorHOUSE®

AuthorHouse™ UK Ltd.
500 Avebury Boulevard
Central Milton Keynes, MK9 2BE
www.authorhouse.co.uk
Phone: 08001974150

First published by AuthorHouse 06/16/2011

ISBN: 978-1-4567-7752-4 (sc)
ISBN: 978-1-4567-7753-1 (e)

ACKNOWLEDGMENTS

Send my regards to those who always, like a candle brightening their surroundings and who are always supportive in times of need.

My compliments to my parents; I hope God gives me the strength to please them, as God's pleasure comes from the priceless gift of parents.

Best compliments to my unique brother, Hassan Salih, and the rest of my family. They have been always behind me and supported me. Also very special thanks to Claudia Cahalane.

PROLOGUE

Early 1940s Florence was a torturously difficult place to be. Striding the two volcanic areas of Mount Vesuvius and the Phlegraean Fields, and sitting by the Gulf of Naples, the city was the most bombed place in Italy during the Second World War. At least two hundred airstrikes took place between 1940 and 1944, and more than twenty thousand civilians lost their lives. Homes were crushed, limbs were lost, and hearts were torn. But the city's people held onto their rich traditions and cultural pursuits as much as possible, finding solace in art and the romantic guitar, preserving as much of their rich architecture as they were able. Business trading continued where it was viable.

As a very rich and somewhat famous Italian merchant living in Florence, Robert Agnoli was pleased with his life and his businesses; he was thankful to still be able to run most of his companies during the war. He had good friends and was known for being gentlemanly to the core. He also gained much respect for his generosity, giving a large part of his wealth to charity. But he prayed every day for the war to end. He wanted his city to return to joy, and he was eager to have a family to share his riches with.

In 1942, a year before the Germans came to occupy the city, Robert met Bella, the love of his life, at a tea dance. While the whole world was low and depressed, Bella's soft rouge lips and her hair, rich in colour like chestnut shells, made Robert sing. He loved her from the moment his body sank into her expressive eyes. Robert visited Bella every day at her family home two streets away, bringing her gifts – green topaz jewellery that matched her clear eyes, poems expressing how she had wrapped herself around his soul and how he never wanted to let her go. She was his life, his true soul mate, and partner. He wanted to be with her until death, give her perfect children to love, and give those children a life where they would want for nothing. He felt strongly that their children should look after his wealth and use it wisely, continuing his support for those less fortunate. He did not want his fortunes squandered and felt that money in the wrong hands could do damage.

Robert believed his wish had been granted when Bella became pregnant with their first child a year later. They had married in a stunning ceremony at their local church, which was being restored following a bomb strike, and now they patiently waited for the new arrival into their family. The couple thought about holding back until the war was over, but they were eager to confirm their lasting love for one another. They were oblivious to the tragedy that was about to hit them.

Two weeks before the baby was due, Bella went into labour and quickly became ill and weak. Her body was not able to do the job of giving birth without taking away all her own strength. She faded and faded until one hour after the baby Antonio was born, and then her life slipped away. When she was pronounced dead, the merchant's devastation was incomprehensible. He fell on his knees, crying like his body had been cut open. He clutched his tiny son to his chest as Bella lay before them. "You are all I have now, Antonio. You have your mother's eyes, her gentle smile. You are her gift to me, and all of your dreams will be fulfilled. I promise." He kissed the boy's forehead and gripped Bella's hand. Without his wife, he saw more war and blood where he'd not noticed it before; she had been his distraction. The cities he visited were in turmoil. Corpses lay everywhere, ravaged by wild animals feasting on them.

Homes lay gutted, windows were blown out, and roofs collapsed. Businesses were derelict, and millions of children, the elderly, and the frail lost their limbs and their sight. The troubles were emphasised even more so by the fact that hundreds of thousands of children were cut off from their families. Many were destined for years full of sadness, and Robert feared for his son's well-being. He didn't want him being brought up in such times without a mother.

However, he did not have to wait too long to give Antonio a more normal life, because the war ended a year later. The elation was immense; people took to the streets to rejoice, holding on to their neighbours for dear life and bursting with relief. Antonio was only one year old, and Robert felt so grateful that his son had not had to suffer the war in his older years and so would not hold on to the deathly and graphic images that had been laid before the world. On the day the war ended, the merchant visited the local salvation church, which was being used as a medical centre for those injured in the war. It was a sparse place, with metal beds and cushions placed wherever there was space. It was clean but basic and grey. The smell of wounds and disinfectant hung in the air as cries of pain filled Robert's ears. He spoke to the nurses about how he could help. Though Robert's parents had died when he was quite young, they had always taught him strong community spirit and concern for others. His father had also visited the sick, and Robert had learned from him. His father had also warned him to look after his wealth because there were people in the world who could not be trusted with such money.

Robert spoke to many of the brave soldiers at the church and quietly expressed his gratitude for their courage and strength, for the sacrifices they'd made for their country, defending it to the end and never giving in to the occupiers. He congratulated them on helping to bring a mean and brutal war to an end. Each soldier told Robert a terrifying story about what had happened to them. He could not imagine the terror they must have been through; it hurt his heart to hear such accounts.

The merchant saw so much heartache at the salvation church, but one sight more than the others had the most profound effect on him – so much so, in fact, that it would change his life forever. As he came towards the corner of the church, on the soiled floor, he saw a small baby, younger than Antonio, sucking on the boot of an unconscious soldier. The child was pale and thin, its clothes grubby and splashed with blood. Robert's stomach felt as though it had been twisted with a wrench. He was frozen to the floor for several moments, and then suddenly with his eyes full of sadness, he cried out, "Why is this baby here?"

The nurses around him explained that they brought the child and its seriously ill mother in earlier that day, after the woman was discovered injured from a bombing. However, they were unable to save the mother, who died two hours later. The baby's father had gone off to war. Robert could have cried a thousand tears for the baby. It was a sight he would never forget.

"We have not yet been able to get this child any milk yet," one of the nurses wailed desperately. "We need to get some very soon." She put her head in her hands, and salty tears began trickling through her fingers and onto the dusty floor.

Robert got closer to the baby and picked her up into his warm arms. He was a strong man with soft hands and a broad frame. The girl immediately gripped him tightly. "This child is so very tired and hungry, I need to help. Please, one of my men will take the little one home, and we will provide milk and shelter." The nurse nodded gratefully, and he passed the child to his most trusted servant.

The nurses were relieved, for they did not have the resources to provide and care for this orphan child. "Is it a boy or a girl?" asked Robert.

"She is a little baby girl, a sweet, dear thing," replied the nurse.

They chatted for a little while and spoke about the care of the baby and her future. Robert was given the little documentation there was about her family before he picked his coat up to leave. "Please let me know if there is anything else I can do," said Robert.

The nurse nodded. "Thank you, sir. I wish you and the baby so much luck."

BEGOTTEN SON: PART ONE
THE PLAN OF THE ITALIAN MERCHANT

"Are you free to come around this evening?" said Robert. He was speaking on the telephone in his study, with his two children in baskets before him. "I need to explain something to you." Two minutes later, Robert put the phone down and then made another call. "Please come around this evening at 6 PM; I must talk to you. He hung up shortly after and sat back. It had been a month since Robert rescued the small girl from the church. The city was jubilant, with sweethearts and children returning to their families. Some didn't come back, of course, and the torment went on for those left behind. But the city was trying to rebuild itself.

Robert looked over to the little one, to whom he has become more and more attached, and gently smiled. He was relieved that she now looked healthier; her skin restored itself to a light olive shade, and her hair was becoming thicker. Antonio and Robert had had many visitors since the baby arrived. Female friends of the family tried to help, and everyone grew to love the baby. She was happy, and her cries were soothed by Robert's affection. Although she had a bad start in life, Robert was determined that she would grow up to be a happy princess. He had invited his two closest friends over for dinner to discuss the future and how he wanted to make this little girl an important part of his life.

At 5.55 PM Bob and Jean arrived, smartly dressed and bearing wine. Bob was a well-known Greek merchant. Whenever there was a problem, he and Robert consulted each other and tried to solve it together. Bob's wife was Italian, and they had a three-year-old daughter, Clara.

Jean Fernand was a Frenchman; he was tall, clever, and young looking, and he managed all of Robert's commercial businesses. He lived in France, Italy, and England and had worked for Robert for five years. He was a trusted friend and colleague who excelled at his work.

"Please come in. Tell me, what I can get you to drink?" Robert said. He asked his housekeeper to prepare something, and the three men sat down. They discussed business for a little while and then moved on to family. Robert excused himself for a few moments and returned with Antonio and the girl in their baskets.

The two men looked at each other questioningly. "Robert, what is going on?" asked Bob.

"My dear friends, I would like your blessing and understanding, and in the future I may need your help. This tiny girl here was at the salvation church last month when I went to visit," he said, picking her up from her basket. "She was in a desolate state, and I felt compelled to bring her home with me." Robert's voice cracked as he remembered the day. "My intention is to bring her up as my own, as Antonio's friend, until a certain age. I want her to feel as special as

Antonio, and I want her to have everything she needs. She has been through so much." He kissed the girl's head, and his eyes crinkled at the corners as she gurgled contentedly.

"This is major news," said Bob. "A very big thing, but I understand why you have done this. You have my utmost respect."

The two men took a sip of their wine and commended Robert on his noble deed. Raising a glass to the child, they offered their support. "Let us name her Rosa, like the most cherished flower," says Bob.

"Wonderful!" said Robert with a smile. "I thank you for this; it will not be easy for us all, but I am glad to have you both on my side. Next, we will set up a new home in the capital city of Rome so that none of the locals in Florence can tell Rosa that she is not really my child," he explained. All the men agreed this is a good idea, and spent the next few days arranging the move to make sure everything was comfortable for the Agnoli family. Jean saw to the financial side of the move and arranged a new home for the family – something surrounded by greenery and with comfortable fixtures and fittings suitable for young children. Everything they needed was in place within a week. Robert, Antonio, and Rosa were accepted into their neighbourhood in Rome within a month or so. The children were adored by locals everywhere they went. They played together for hours, with Antonio being protective towards the young Rosa. Over time, they started their education and made many new friends, while Robert became acquainted with some upstanding members of the local community, including men of the church and of the law, and shop keepers and business owners in the area. Life was just right for them all.

But, unfortunately, Robert's plan for the children's future meant that he must keep them apart as much as possible until they were adults. Therefore a year before they were due to start school, he called Jean and talked to him about the possibility of Antonio staying with him in England during term time, while Rosa stayed home in Italy. Robert didn't want to be without Antonio, but he saw it as the only way.

Jean was very happy to have the young boy stay with him and treated Antonio like a king's son . He created a magnificent room for Robert's son, with all his favourite things and photos of Robert and Rosa to remind him of home. Antonio was happy and made many new friends in England, enjoying English traditions and culture. However, he always looked forward to the school holidays, when he could return home to his family.

As he got older, he would sometimes bring English friends back to stay in Italy for a few weeks, and they would play while Rosa spent time with her own school friends. They all got together for a lovely family meal at night and talked about what they had done that day.

The two children had excellent schooling and were very gifted at their studies; they worked hard to achieve good results, always encouraged by Robert. They passed all their exams each year and then went on to university. In their early twenties, Antonio graduated from the College of Commerce in Britain, and Rosa qualified as a civil engineer in Italy. Robert was overwhelmed with pride.

After his graduation ceremony, Antonio returned back to

Italy to manage his father's commercial businesses with Jean. They made a perfect team, and Robert was very pleased. He wished Bella could have seen how well their boy had turned out. Rosa was also working locally, and Robert was equally happy with her for maturing into a fine young woman.

Jean had lots to teach Antonio, and they spent many hours at the office each day. At the end of one particularly busy week, Jean and Antonio sat in the office surrounded by books and papers, combing through all elements of the German side of the business so that Antonio could see how things worked there.

There were a lot of details, and they had been there for eight hours already. Antonio's eyes were burning a little from exhaustion, and he kept rubbing them. He paused for a couple of moments and stared out of the window.

"Are you okay?" inquired Jean, who was more used to long hours in the office.

"Um, yes. I, er …" he couldn't finish his sentence. He wanted to ask Jean some questions about his personal life; after all this time, he didn't know much about Jean's love life. He felt there was a bit of a barrier between them.

"What is it?" Jean asked.

"No, it's nothing," said Antonio, nervously looking back down at his notes.

"You can ask me what you like, Antonio," Jean replied.

"I was just wondering. I saw a lot of different women at the house growing up, but I never knew which ones you really loved," said Antonio, sounding genuinely puzzled.

"Well, I do love someone, but it is hard to be with her," said Jean, as though he was resigning himself to unhappiness.

"Can I help you at all?" asked Antonio sympathetically.

"Let's talk about it another time. But I have some things I need to tell you about women," says Jean, changing the subject and trying to be more light-hearted.

Antonio looked curious. He was happy at not having to work for a little while.

"There are lessons to be learned, young man," Jean said with a laugh. "Never use the word 'fine' to describe how a woman looks; this will cause you to have an argument."

"Really?" said Antonio, looking bemused.

"Yes, and of course, you must never, ever say you don't like the way she looks. Another thing is, if a woman says she will be five minutes getting ready, she will be at least half an hour.

"Haha! Why do they have to take so long?" laughed Antonio. "What else do I need to know?"

Jean continued. "Okay, so if you've upset a woman, and you ask what's wrong and she says nothing, she does not mean nothing; she is very pissed off at you and is probably contemplating her revenge. Next, if you ask if you can do something, and she raises her eyebrow and says, 'Go ahead,' that means don't do it unless you want to end up in another argument." Jean obviously spoke from a lot of bitter experience.

Antonio was intrigued. "You have learned a lot; I'm surprised you still like women!"

"That is the magic of women," said Jean. "You never know what they want, but you always want them."

"What about us men, Jean . How should we communicate our feelings to women?" Antonio asked.

"We are much more direct," said Jean. "A man will just say, 'Don't worry about it' if he just doesn't want to listen or feels let down, or …"

At that point, a member of the staff entered the room. "Sir, one of the merchants has just arrived from Germany. He would like to see you."

"Excuse me," said Jean to Antonio, and he left the room.

In some ways, Robert couldn't believe how quickly time was passing. His children's childhood had disappeared before his eyes, and now, with them both back in Italy and grown up, he knew it was time to reveal the truth to them about Rosa's identity and about his plan for them. It was a day he had thought about for so many years, and it filled him with panic, but there was no more time to waste.

The merchant invited Bob and Jean to his home for a few days so that he could talk to them about what he was going to do. He spent the next two days mulling everything over in his mind until they arrived. "I am so relieved to see you both," Robert said, hugging them tightly. His face looked pale and drawn.

"What is it Robert? You look terrible," said Bob. The two could tell Robert was not his usual happy self, though his face quickly lit up when they arrived. He felt calmer with them there.

"It is late, and you have been travelling for many hours. Please, take a rest for half an hour, as we are likely to have a late night. There is much to talk about," he said.

Later they met in Robert's dining room and stayed up

very late discussing the future. They put together a full plan on how to explain the situation to Antonio and Rosa and also to help them understand the plans Robert had put together for them to secure all of their futures and his wealth. "I am worried, I admit," says Robert. "I don't know how they will react; I have been thinking about this day for so long."

"Robert," said Bob, "they know you always have their best interests at heart. That is all they can ask for. It will be okay." After many hours, the two guests retired to their rooms and slept deeply for a few hours. Robert spent the night tossing and turning, unable to relax. He kept thinking about what he was going to say the next day.

The next morning, Bob woke up early, got washed and dressed, and then walked across the corridor to Antonio's room. He knocked on the young man's bedroom door and saw Antonio shaving at his sink. "Come in," Antonio shouted, tapping his razor under the running water to clean it.

Bob pushed the door open slowly. Antonio walked closer to him, wiped his face and hands with a towel, and extended his hand to Bob. "How do you do?" He didn't recognise the man but knew that he must be one of the friends who arrived to see his father last night.

Bob hugged Antonio and smiled, looking the young man up and down. "I'm Bob. When I last saw you, you were only one year old .Do you remember that?"

Antonio laughed gently. "No, but it's great to meet you now. I have heard all about you from my father and sister. About how bright you are, and how successful you are at your work. I am honoured."

"That is most kind," said Bob. "But your father is one of

the most loyal and respected men in the community. He is the person I look up to." The two chatted for a few minutes about the past and present, and then Antonio mentioned the future. Bob coughed and was a little agitated. "I have to go now, but before you go to work, I would like to see you and your friend, Rosa downstairs," he says.

Antonio looks questioningly. "Friend?"

"Well," said Bob, "We are all each other's friends, aren't we?" He closed Antonio's door behind him, quickly disappearing down the stairs and joining Robert and Jean in Robert's meeting room to have breakfast. They chatted amongst themselves, waiting for the two children and eating some eggs and fruit.

A short while later, Rosa and Antonio flung the door open, laughing and joking to each other. "My dear father," said Antonio, "you have asked us to come down for an important matter. What is it?" He recovered from his laugh and looked sincerely at Robert.

"Yes, my son, please sit down," Robert said, ushering them to sit opposite him as they always did for serious discussions. They looked at each other nervously, sensing their father was stressed.

Robert bowed his head and stood up from his chair, pacing the room. "Rosa, Antonio, you know how much I love you both." The two looked at each other again, confusion across their faces. Robert continued, "I've been trying my best to provide all you need in life. And now that you've grown up, I must explain something to you. I'm getting old and have no idea how long this earth will take me for. I want you to know the secrets before I die.

Bob and Jean listened intently, struggling to hear Robert's hushed tones.

Antonio was now panicking about his father's health. "Father, are you okay? If this is about your will and your wealth, we are not worried; it's not important," he said in a hurried voice, interrupting his father.

"My dear father, you are ill, but you are too scared to tell us – I knew it," said Rosa anxiously. You have been so down these last few weeks."

"No, no, my daughter," Robert replied to her with a strained smile.

"Well, then, are you going away for a long time?" she uttered questioningly, clutching at ideas and looking perplexed.

Jean found the tension unbearable. "Your father has something very important to tell you; we are here to witness what he has to say."

"Just tell us what's going on please, Father!" said Antonio, sounding impatient.

"I'm sure whatever it is will be fine," Rosa joined in. They were both innocent to the fact that their lives were both about to dramatically change forever.

"Rosa," said Robert, trying to sound calm. "I need to tell you something. It is very difficult for me." He paused for a long while and took a deep breath before letting out a long sigh. "You are not my child." Robert looked at his feet and then up at Rosa. Her cheeks were losing colour as she sat unable to speak, with a mouth so dry it could sand a table. Antonio reached out his hand and held hers. Robert continued in a low voice. "Antonio was just a baby when the war ended; it was a terrible time, and so many bad things happened. I tried to do what I could for our community and went to visit the local salvation church to offer my support. It was there I saw the most heartbreaking scene. You were there, Rosa, all alone beside injured soldiers. I wanted to help you, and so I brought you home," he finished, tears in his eyes.

"Oh Father, Father. Why was I there?" Rosa said desperately, her eyes like a frightened animal, petrified of its fate.

"Rosa, I'm so sorry to tell you, your mother died in a bombing, and your father went to war and never returned. It is so very tragic."

Rosa sobbed into Antonio's shoulder while Robert, Jean, and Bob moved closer to them for support.

"Your father did a very noble thing," said Bob. "He took you to make a good life for you."

"Forgive me for not telling you until now," Robert cried. "I wanted you to always feel the same as Antonio. You are both equally special to me." The five of them talked for hours about what had happened and why Robert took the children to Rome and how he didn't want Rosa to know the news in her childhood, so as not to upset her.

Rosa did not know what to think. She understood her father's decision not to tell her, but now she felt so lonely and lost. She wondered about her mother and father, her history. Who was she? She felt empty, as though her whole life had been a pretence. However, she was yet to hear the most shocking part. Neither she nor Antonio was prepared for what would come from their father's mouth next.

Robert's maid brought them tea, and Robert took another

deep breath while pouring it. His hand was shaking. "Rosa, Antonio." He took a moment and looked straight at them. "There is also something else I need to tell you. I have always planned that the two of you will marry each other and take care of our wealth and do good things with it." Rosa dropped her cup on the table and sat with an open mouth. The cup fell to the floor and cracked. The room was in stark silence for what seemed like a lifetime. "You are not brother and sister, and I want you to marry in accordance with my will, which Jean and Bob have witnessed. That is my plan for you." The two men nodded at the children.

Rosa and Antonio were sweating and shivering while listening to Robert's words.

Antonio was embarrassed, and his voice shook. "Father, that is not possible because we have been brother and sister all our lives. We are not romantic with each other; it does not make sense. All our friends and the whole community in the city know us as siblings. What will people say to us? A brother and sister marrying is totally against our religion – we will be condemned, our reputation, and yours, will be destroyed! This is insane."

"This is not right," Rosa blurted. "Why have we not been told of this before?"

"It really was in your best interest," said Jean. "Believe us, this has not been easy for your father. We have all thought for hours, months, and years thinking about all this."

Bob got closer to Antonio and quietly said to him: "Do not worry, Antonio, we have thought of everything; this really is the best thing, I promise."

Antonio was seething with anger at being told he should

do something like this against his will. He was not normally an angry sort of person, but he was in deep shock. He got up from his seat and pushed his chair away, before turning to Bob. "I am leaving. Do not ever speak about this again." He stormed out of the room.

"I will talk to him later," said Robert. He then put his hands on Rosa's face and kissed her on both cheeks and on her forehead. "You are the most important woman in my life, and I have wanted to tell you the truth for so long, but I had to wait until I thought you were ready. I want only the best for you, my daughter." His face looked pained.

Rosa put her head down and began to cry uncontrollably. Her mind was racing, her life in pieces. Robert and his two friends solemnly left the room, reassuring him that his wishes would be granted. They wanted to give Rosa time on her own to consider her life and her future.

Rosa and Antonio spent the next few days thinking over everything, feeling deeply uncomfortable about these shards of glass which have been dropped into their lives. They thought of each other as brother and sister and were embarrassed to be anything else to each other. They withdrew from each other and their friends, unable to reveal what was going on. They felt lonely and uncertain about everything. Rosa's friends called her and wrote to her, but she did not know what to say.

Robert's vision, which he drew up with his friends, was done so because he wanted to ensure that no outsiders took his wealth. He knew that this was commonplace if a family did not have a watertight plan for their future and for any inheritance. He wanted to ensure that it all went to Antonio, and he believed because he had brought up Rosa as his own too, he could trust them both to keep the money in the Agnoli family for him. His heart was always in the right place, but at first it was very difficult for them to understand this. The situation was highly complex.

Over the following days, tempers slowly began to settle, eventually Rosa and Antonio started to speak to their father and each other. They were thinking hard about how they could achieve their father's vision, because they loved him and wanted to please him.

Antonio was well-known in Rome for being a quiet, loyal, and an understanding person. He had his place in the heart of city's people and was known to be the son of the rich merchant .He was seen as being just like his father, always trying to help others. But he did not feel people would believe that Rosa and he were not brother and sister, and he knew that local religious leaders would prohibit a brother and sister marrying. There would be terrible consequences if such a thing was found to have happened.

After several weeks, Antonio approached Robert in his study one morning. "Father, Rosa and I have spoken in great detail about what you have said. Please understand that this will not be easy for us, but we will try, with all our energies, to do as you wish. I know you only want the best, and I hope we can make you happy."

Robert looked kindly at his son. "I do understand this Antonio. I know it won't be easy, but when it is all complete, there is a glorious life waiting for you both."

Antonio nodded; he tried to be convinced by Robert's words, but apprehension still showed on his face. He went back to his room and lied on his bed feeling numb.

For two years the children remained in Rome and tried to work out a way to fulfil their father's dream, but they knew deep down it was hopeless. Eventually, after a deep discussion late one night, they decided to go overseas to think about their lives and to try to be together without any questions. Antonio and Rosa knew they would miss Robert, and he would find it difficult without them, but they could see no other way. They were trying to change their relationship with each other, day by day.

Robert was very happy to hear this news, but he was also concerned about them being without him for what could prove to be quite a long time. He was used to having them around him and liked to protect Rosa and Antonio. He loved seeing them regularly and spending time with them; they were a close family. But he accepted their decision to go and achieve his aim in any way they could. In the following days, Robert thought long and hard about his children's trip until he struck upon what he believed was a very bright idea. It was an idea which could involve much work, but it could help shape Rosa and Antonio's lives in the way he intended.

Robert sent messages to Bob and Jean to help him. When Jean received the news, he said he was pleased to support in any way he could, and he then went to Bob's house to discuss what assistance could be provided.

But Bob was much older than Jean and was getting ill. The years were creeping up on him, his skin was taught, and his legs were heavy; he struggled to travel much these days. Because he had promised Robert for so many years that he would be a loyal friend and help him achieve his dream, he offered his only daughter in his place. Clara, his girl, was a beautiful, elegant, and bright law graduate from Greece. She had a strong sense of adventure and was always moving around. She loved her independence, but her father was her number one priority and she was always keen to please him.

She followed her father's orders and went straight to Robert's house in Italy to help Rosa and Antonio. Jean arrived soon after, and they both received an extremely warm welcome from the Agnoli family. Rosa and Antonio were getting ready to leave in a few days, but Robert had made them wait until his two friends arrived. They all began working together immediately to flesh out Robert's plan in detail. They spent hours and hours in the meeting room, with streams of paper work before them and a supply of food and drink regularly brought by Robert's staff.

The plans were intricate and, crucially, would involve a lookalike being found for either Rosa or Antonio. Everyone was amazed at Robert's bright mind – they all agreed the plan was perfect, a work of genius. But it would involve absolute attention to detail in order to succeed, and a degree of luck.

Rosa and Antonio prepared themselves for the first step. With the help of Clara and Jean, they would search different countries around the world in order to find Rosa or Antonio's lookalike, and then the other steps of the plan would follow.

The next day Rosa and Antonio packed their things and arranged everything for their travels. They were excited to see so many different countries and cities across the world; to experience new places, new sights, and sounds; and to be going together. But there was anxiety too, about fulfilling their mission. About being away from all their friends, their hometown, and their father.

"Here, take this money for whatever you need," said Robert as they tried to eat some breakfast rolls and tea in the dining area on the morning of leaving. He sat with them for a moment, but no one was really hungry because they were too nervous.

"Thank you, Father," said Antonio.

"We will spend it wisely," added Rosa, smiling warmly and touching Robert's hand. She would miss her father so much.

Robert was very emotional when they left late morning – he had tears in his eyes as they said good-bye. "I do not know when I will see you again, my children, but I hope we will be reunited before too much time passes. I will think of your goodness and your radiant smiles," he said while he wept quietly.

As they sat in the back of their car, heading to the airport, Rosa and Antonio held hands and felt some kind of spark for the first time. They both knew that their feelings towards each other were starting to change. The thoughts of being brother and sister were very gradually starting to fade. Antonio put his arm around Rosa and held her close while they sat in silence. They arrived at the airport two hours before their flight to France was due, and they sat and drank coffee and stared out of the window at the planes arriving. They didn't speak much but felt close to each other and had a sense of comfort. They kept their eyes out when people passed, to see if anyone matched their appearance.

"What if we don't find anyone?" asked Rosa.

"We will," replied Antonio. He himself was unsure, but he did not want to tell Rosa this. He put his hand through Rosa's hair. "Think of how many millions of people are in the world. Of course we'll find someone. Please don't worry. Don't forget, Clara and Jean are also looking."

While Antonio and Rosa set off to explore Europe, Clara and Jean decided to move between a number of other countries, including Australia and America, doing some business at the same time. They brought photos of Antonio and Rosa with them and searched for lookalikes all over. They also sent copies of the photos to merchants they'd worked with in other countries, offering them rewards and good business if they could help track down anyone who looked like either of the two Agnoli children. Meanwhile Rosa and Antonio's love for one another was deepening. They were beginning to long for each other in their heart and loins, enjoying long meals together by candlelight in Paris and strolling along the Champs-Élysées hand in hand, absorbing the romance of the city. Neither of them had felt so strongly about anyone before, but they took their time to talk about their love, finding it difficult to put it into words.

Antonio gave Rosa much attention. He adored her and made sure that everything she wanted was attended to. He felt closer to her every day and understood what she wanted more deeply. They shared their dreams and thoughts with each other, without explicitly saying they were in love with each other. Their feelings made them even more determined to carry out their father's plan and be together properly. They stayed in France for six weeks, hopelessly looking in all the major cities, but alas, they could find absolutely no one who matched their description. On the seventh week they decided they would move on to Turkey and then explore the neighbouring country of Iran. They packed up and set off again.

In Turkey there were some political troubles, but they find room to enjoy the beauty, swimming in the stunning Aegean sea together, visiting the breathtaking mountains of the Afyon province, and sampling the local Turkish delight sweets. But their search did not bring the desired outcome, and Antonio was becoming desperate. Rosa was the first thing he thought about each morning and the last thing he thought of at night, and he wanted to be with her properly. They had met a couple of people who showed some resemblance to them, but they knew none would be convincing enough to friends and family who knew them well. After another six weeks, they took their final trip to the hot springs in Pamukkale, and from there they were offered a lift with a new friend, into Iran. It was a long way to travel – more than a day of driving – but their friend was appreciative of their company during his lengthy journey to deliver some important documents.

It was a time of massive urban growth in Iran, a country the size of Britain, France, Spain, and Germany put together. There were many towns and cities to visit. The two searched for hours every day, going through Tehran, Isfahan, Ahvaz, Qom, and Mashhad. They constantly tried to lift their spirits, reassuring each other that they would eventually find someone.

Merchants working in Iraq and Syria had been sent photos of the two and were offered rewards to help them with their mission. But this avenue was also proving fruitless. They moved on to Cyprus and Greece, exploring the all the islands. There was much political unrest again, and it was difficult to move about too much without constantly being questioned by the authorities. Rosa and Antonio didn't stay too long before going to Germany. By this time they had heard that Clara and Jean had now also tried several other countries including Russia, Poland, and Romania, and they had reached a dead-end at every port. Everyone was running out of hope, but they were too scared to tell each other. They updated Robert every week but had nothing concrete to report back to him. Rosa and Antonio consoled each other that they were not yet able to please their beloved father. They wanted to talk to each other about how they were feeling but often just sat and hugged one another for ages, saying nothing. Rosa felt deeply adored by Antonio and was happy that he lavished her with warmth and attention. He was her rock.

As they sat in a restaurant in Germany late one summer evening, Rosa suggested they write down their feelings for each other. This, she thought, would help them overcome their shyness. She took a notepad and pen out of her bag and laid it on the table. She smiled and started scribbling quickly: "I'm so happy when your warm eyes smile at me. I think of you all the time." She passed it to Antonio and looked expectantly at him.

He read her words with his heart beating faster and feeling nervous, but he couldn't help grinning. He thought for a few minutes about what to write back. Rosa went to the ladies' room to compose herself and give Antonio some time. "Your warmth and generous nature makes my heart leap," he wrote back and left the paper for Rosa to see. His face felt hot.

When Rosa read it, she looked into his eyes intensely for several minutes, fixated. He stared back and held her hands in his for what seems like an eternity, and then they continued writing, filling up the entire page and stopping only momentarily to gaze at each other and stroke one another's face. Once the page was full, Rosa turned it over and wrote in big letters, "You are my soulmate. I want to be yours forever."

Antonio read the words and took a deep breath before leaning across the table. "My wonderful Rosa, I feel the same," he said out loud, and then he kissed her gently. Their faces were alight like a full moon in pitch black sky.

"You aren't supposed to talk!" she joked.

"Talk?" he replied. "I want to sing and scream with excitement." They hugged again and held on to each other tightly. The other people in the restaurant stared, but they did not mind.

The next day, after a long sleep and lucid dreams about each other, they walked hand in hand around the city of Hamburg, going into restaurants and cafes, trying to find out who they should talk to locally that might have a good network. While they talked to one cafe owner and handed him some photos of themselves, a man tapped Antonio on the shoulder. "What are you looking for, son? You seem desperate," he said, sounding like he wanted to help.

"Please, sir, we are Italian. We were cut off from our relations during the war, and we are hoping to find them once more to reunite our families," said Antonio hopefully.

"Well, I'm a merchant, been here since I moved from Spain ten years ago, and I know a lot of people. If you want to give me some of your photos, I will do my best for you; you seem like nice people. It must be hard to not be united with your family."

The Spanish merchant sat with them for a while, looking at them and looking at their photos while sipping coffee. "Ahh," he said suddenly, staring directly into Rosa's eyes. "There is a girl I remember I met at a restaurant in Madrid last year who looked like you. She worked there while doing her studies." Antonio and Rosa were so happy they could have burst with joy.

They stayed for a while longer drinking tea and coffee, and then they paid the merchant's bill before heading off.

They contacted Clara and Jean to meet them the next day in the restaurant to see if Rosa's lookalike really did exist.

Then they called Robert and could hear the anticipation in his voice. He had been waiting every week for some good news like this, and when he put the phone down, he opened some of his favourite wine to celebrate. He felt more relaxed and hopeful now that his plans might eventually come together while he was still young enough to see to his estate properly.

That night Rosa and Antonio slept very soundly; they were the happiest they had been for a while. In the morning, they dressed quickly and left for Madrid. Upon arrival, the two skipped through the city at lunchtime, hopeful that their search might soon be over. The Spanish merchant was so insistent that Rosa had a twin sister working at the restaurant, and they'd taken him at his word because they had truly wanted to believe it. He seemed to be a very genuine man. They sat down outside the restaurant and ordered some wine, their eyes searching for the lookalike. They watched all the staff, and Rosa went into the restaurant to look around, but they found nothing. Forty-five minutes later, a young girl arrived with a rucksack, and she had exactly the same hair as Rosa. Antonio gasped as they watched the girl disappear into the restaurant. "It must be her Rosa," shouted Antonio, a little too loudly.

"Shh, we need to keep calm, we need to see her face." Ten minutes later the girl reappeared with her work uniform on.

But as she gets closer to them, they are in disbelief. She is the same height and weight as Rosa and had similar hair, but her facial features bore little no resemblance. "She is nothing like my beautiful Rosa," Antonio said with a frown. "This is ridiculous!"

Rosa felt as though she would not be able to go on with the search after this disappointment. Her eyes were heavy, she was dizzy, and she quickly fell into Antonio's arms, starting to cry. "I want to give up, Antonio. This is never going to work," she sobbed. She began hyperventilating and having a panic attack.

"Rosa please, calm down," said Antonio, feeling very stressed and self-conscious that everyone was looking at them. He held her tightly as her body went limp and she fainted. Everyone crowded around with water and tissues, but Antonio tried to disperse the situation by telling people that Rosa was very exhausted and did not like crowds. He wiped her moist brow with his shirt, and she started to come around a little. He gave her a big gulp of water and held her tightly.

Jean and Clara arrived at this point, and they all took Rosa back to their hotel to discuss the situation. The two lovers were frustrated that the first step of Robert's plans had still not come together, meaning that they could move forward.

While Rosa rested, the others talked, and Jean suggests that Antonio and Rosa go to London for a number of reasons. Firstly, because London was a very crowded city, and so it would be easy for them to settle and be together there without people finding out their secret. Also, Robert did a lot of business in the United Kingdom, and it would be more simple for them to all see each other. They could also take over Robert's business in Britain.

When Rosa awoke and they explained the plan to her, she felt hopeful again and was happy that she and Antonio can be together more as a couple in London.

Robert was relieved when they told him. However, he was worried that so much time had passed, and still the first stage of his plan had yet to materialise. They assured him that they would keep searching. It was decided that Clara and Jean would go with them and act as assistants in whatever they needed to do.

A few days later, they headed to London and booked into the very private Dorchester Hotel, where they knew they would be treated well. It was a fresh start for them all, and Rosa and Antonio felt more comfortable knowing they would have a stable base for a while.

For the first few weeks, Rosa and Antonio took daily tours around London with their assistants, so they could get to know the city better and also forget their worries for a while. They were in much need of a break, and so they wander around and admired the beautiful views, particularly enjoying St Paul's Cathedral and the Tower of London. "It's such a striking city, Antonio; it must have been fascinating growing up in the UK," said Rosa.

"It's true. English people have great strength, and the place is so historical. There are many tales to tell about England, my love, and I have a lifetime to tell you. I will take you to some of the places Jean took me when I was student."

They spent hours walking along the River Thames, enjoying the water and the grand architecture and the very busy docks that surrounded it. They were both amazed by the number of people in London – more than seven million. They felt it would be an easy place to be anonymous.

The couple regularly visited Robert's offices and work sites so that Antonio could understand his father's business in these countries. It was the perfect arrangement. After a month in the city, Antonio called a meeting with the two assistants.

"Clara, Jean," he said calmly, "I know now what needs to be done here with the businesses. I think it would be okay if you go back to your own work; I can handle it now." They agreed, for they were not really needed until a lookalike was found.

Rosa and Antonio also found a house to buy. They wanted somewhere central to the businesses but that would be quiet sometimes and amongst nature, away from the hustle and bustle. They stayed away from the eastern side of the city, which had bombed during the war, instead looked in west London, the more affluent areas, before discovering their perfect home on the edge of Battersea Park in South London.

It was a tranquil, romantic setting but was still near the main thrust of the city. The birds sang in the morning, and children played in the afternoon. Rosa and Antonio were happy with the house and decided they wanted to buy it. But first they needed to secure the money at the bank.

They decided to go to the city centre the next day to arrange the finances. Clara and Jean would go with them to make sure everything was okay, and they also wanted to buy some things to take back home.

"Let's leave straight after breakfast," said Antonio. "Rosa, maybe you could go to the bank with Clara to discuss the money, and I could go with Jean to the market to help him pick up what they need to take home?"

The next day, they took a taxi into town and got out near the main bank at Trafalgar Square. "Will you be okay, Rosa?" inquired Antonio.

"Yes, don't worry. But please don't be long, in case I need you later," she said.

"We will be quick, I promise," Antonio said with a smile. He felt a flush of excitement that he and Rosa would soon be together in their own home. They parted ways, and Rosa and Clara make their way into the huge building.

"Good afternoon, can I help you?" a member of staff asked as they pushed the main door open.

The assistant was tall with tight, curly black hair and a helpful face. "Yes, can I see somebody? I need £35,000 to buy a house, and I need it quickly," said Rosa assertively. She was on a mission and wanted to get the money sorted as speedily as possible. She quickly scanned the room to see if there was someone more important she should be speaking to.

"Madam, that is a very large sum of money, do you know that?" replied the assistant.

"I do indeed," said Rosa. "But I have the money, and I have identification."

The man smiled and became extra helpful. "No problem, I will see the bank manager immediately." He walked off and then returned, looking flustered. "Sorry, could I please take your name and address so that I can deal with your inquiry properly?"

"Of course," says Rosa, writing her father's address on a sheet of notepaper before handing it to the assistant.

"Thank you, madam, thank you very much. I will sort this out for you," he said, vanishing into a back office.

Rosa joined Clara on some chairs in the waiting area in the corner, and they chatted for a moment about Rosa's relationship with Antonio and how it had changed. Clara was keen to know more, but within a few minutes, the staff member returned and called Rosa into the manager's office.

"Follow me," he said, pointing down the hallway. Rosa happily walked with him to the end of the corridor and was left outside the door to let herself in. She knocked.

"Come in, please," a male voice said. Rosa pressed her hand on the door to open it —and the sight she saw almost knocked her off her feet. She looked straight at the manager, dumbstruck. "What is it?" said the bank manager, getting up from his seat and looking concerned. Rosa's face was red and she was shaking. He took her hand and led her to a seat. "Madam, what is wrong? Do you need some water? Do you need medical attention?"

She looked at him blankly and was speechless for several minutes before exclaiming, "Oh my god. Oh my dear god!" She repeated the words over and over again.

The manager made her drink some water, and she inhaled several deep breaths, trying to calm herself down. "You, you have the same face as my brother. Yes, the same face, exactly the same face," she shouted joyously, looking up to the heavens as if to thank God. She could not believe her eyes.

After so long, she wasn't sure if she was imagining what she saw before her. Was this really Antonio's lookalike? She ran from the office, calling back to the manager, "I will bring my brother now."

Clara saw her dart out from the corner of her eye, and she leapt out of her seat to chase after her. "Rosa, Rosa! What's happening?" she yelled in a puzzled voice.

Rosa did not stop; she launched into the street and called out for Antonio. Luckily he was just across the street with Jean, walking in her direction. When he saw her, he began to run to her. She launched herself at him and hugged him with all her strength. "Antonio, oh my god, you will not believe it. I have found your lookalike. The bank manager I have just seen is your exact double!" She jumps up and down, laughing deliriously.

"Are you serious? Really?" asked Antonio. He could hardly speak himself, and his head was cloudy with excitement. "Wow, wow, oh wow. I feel like I am dreaming." Antonio ran up and down the street like a footballer who had just scored a goal in the World Cup.

Clara finally caught up, panicking and grabbing hold of Jean. "What is going on?" she asked him.

"I don't know! You were with her. Why do you not know?" he asked.

Rosa explained what she saw as best she can, mixing her words with disbelief. "The bank manager I've just seen, he is Antonio's twin, I swear. You cannot imagine someone looking more like him in your wildest dreams!" She laughed.

"My eyes?" said Antonio.

"Yes!" she replied.

"My nose, mouth?"

"Yes!"

Jean joined in. "Is he the same height? Does he have the same hair, the same voice?" he spoke quickly with wide eyes.

Rosa tried to calm herself and catch her breath. "He looks similar in height, I think. Similar voice, nearly, but his hair is a little different."

"That's the easiest thing to sort out. Fantastic!" said Clara, beaming. "We can do the hair, no problem. This is such good news after all this time. We need to celebrate this; it marks a big change for all of us. Life will be different now. We can finally move forward."

Jubilant, they took a car back to Jean and Clara's hotel for celebratory drinks, and so the two assistants could arrange to stay at the hotel indefinitely.

Rosa and Antonio sat in the hotel lounge, breathing heavy sighs of relief as though a mighty weight had been lifted from their shoulders.

Jean arrived with a bottle of the hotel's best champagne and poured them all a glass. 'Here's to the future," he said in an upbeat voice, and they all raised their glasses and then discussed what to do next and how they would lure the manager.

Jean put his hands on Antonio's shoulders and looked at Rosa. "Don't forget, you are brother and sister, right? Nothing else, okay? This must be executed absolutely perfectly."

"We understand, Jean, I promise," said Antonio, smiling gently at Rosa.

Jean also told Antonio he should act as though he had a chronic stutter and preferred not to talk. This way, the manager and Rosa could get to know each other and form a relationship – at least a relationship in the manager's eyes – without Antonio having to get involved too much. It would also mean that people could easily distinguish between Antonio and the manager, which was an important part of the plan.

Antonio agreed, although he knew this would be difficult, and then he and Rosa left to go back to the bank.

When Rosa and Antonio entered the bank, all the staff stared at Rosa, thinking she was mad in some way for running out of the place several hours earlier.

But as soon as they saw Antonio, they were all dumbfounded. "Wow," they whispered. "The manager has a twin," said one. "How strange."

Rosa ushered Antonio straight to the manager's office, where they found him sitting back at his desk and filling in some forms. He looked up. "Can I help …" he started before he saw Antonio's face, practically his own face, staring at him. Both Antonio and his double gazed at each other, astounded at how anyone could look quite as similar as this. They studied each other intensely, and after a little while the manager put his hand through his hair and squeezed his hands tightly together. "God, this is so strange. Unbelievable," he gasped. Antonio was mesmerised but forced himself not to talk. He was struggling and thinking of Jean's advice over and over.

"I'm Alex," the manger said to Rosa while still fixated on Antonio. He then shook Antonio's hand without speaking, studying all his features in detail.

"I, I, uh, ah," Antonio stuttered. He kept opening and shutting his eyes and nodding his head. He pushed his foot into the floor as he tried to get his words out.

Alex laughed and looked confused, but Rosa quickly interrupted, "I'm sorry, this is my brother, Antonio – he was born with an acute stammer. He finds it extremely difficult to get his words out. Please do not joke about this; it is very difficult for him."

"Oh, I am so sorry." Alex held his red face in his hands; he felt awful. "Please sit down." He pulled out some chairs for Antonio and Rosa. "Can I get you some coffee?" He phoned his receptionist to bring the drinks.

Rosa and Alex wasted no time in chatting about this amazing coincidence for several minutes, getting to know each other more and discussing both their histories and childhoods.

Alex was originally from America, but he left the country without his parents when he was fifteen years old. He was now in his late twenties, the same age as Rosa and Antonio. The only different between the two men was that Antonio's hair was black, coarse and short, whereas Alex's was much softer and in a long, flowing style. Alex also had a very noticeable scar on his left hand, of which all his friends were very aware. He'd fallen off a motorbike as a teenager and skidded down an embankment. He broke several bones, but the scar was the only visible reminder of the accident.

Alex was an astute and intellectual person. He was very capable in his job and had risen through the ranks quickly after taking a degree in economics. He was promoted frequently, but he was a hard manager and did not have many fans amongst his staff. He was easily irritated by them and would lose control of his temper, making them were scared of him.

Three strong coffees and two hours later, their discussion of the lookalikes and Rosa and Antonio's financial request was over. Alex agreed to sort the money out for them the very next day.

The lovers then left the bank feeling positive about the future, and they had to stop themselves hugging and kissing each other excitedly in the street.

When they returned to the hotel, they all spoke to Robert on the phone to tell him the great news. They explained how Clara and Jean would now stay to assist with the next part of the plan. Robert had been feeling stressed the last few weeks and had struggled to sleep, but he felt much better after hearing the news. He even gave a large sum of money to the local hospitals and schools to thank God.

Then Clara, Jean, and the two lovers looked in detail at the second step of the plan, drawn up by Robert. Once again, they stayed in their hotel suite at the table until the early hours of the morning, mapping everything out.

The next day, Rosa took a long walk into the bank to think about everything. When she arrived, Alex was waiting with the money. He smiled when he saw her and held her hand for several moments as he placed the envelope containing the cash into it. He looked into her eyes and said, "I wish you the best of luck with everything. It has been a pleasure to meet you." He would not let go of her hand.

"Alex … may I call you that?" she asked.

"Of course," came the upbeat reply.

"I would like to thank you for sorting all this out so quickly and kindly for us. My brother and I are so grateful to you; it means very much." She handed him some paper and held his hand. "Here is our address and number, if you would like to stay in touch."

Alex could not hide his elation that this beautiful young woman was giving him so much attention. He grinned widely and felt warmth in his body. "I will do that," he responded. The seeds were sown, and it was obvious that Alex had taken an interest in Rosa.

The next step of the plan was for the manager to become completely and utterly smitten with Rosa's charms. He should fall deeply in love with the beautiful Italian.

Rosa's obvious wealth should help attract him, they thought. Alex was very drawn to money and power, and this made him quite ruthless in the way he treated staff. He never gave them any time off because he was concerned about it interfering with profits. Any mistakes were punished without a thought, and money was deducted from wages when he felt it necessary.

But despite all this, he had managed to become an object of desire for his beautiful, blond secretary, Emma. She was crazy about Alex and thought about him often. She would follow him around and cater to his every whim, waiting for him to return her desire.

From the moment she had started working at the bank a year ago, she believed Alex would eventually be her lover and husband, and they would have a family together one day. She would sit at her desk for hours fantasising about their future lives together – their home, their children, everything.

But the thing was, Alex despised her and wanted her out of her job and out of his life. He was not interested in her looks, her voice, her disposition, or anything about her. He wished she would leave him alone. He'd had girlfriends similar to her in the past and had never gotten on well with them. Rosa seemed to be much more his kind of woman.

Two days later, Rosa was in the study at the new house, drinking tea and looking out to the park, when the phone rang. "Hello?" she answered.

"Hi, is this Rosa?" came the voice.

Rosa recognised the caller's American twang straight away. "Hello there, Alex, how nice to hear from you. How have you been?"

They chatted for about twenty minutes before Alex mentioned the idea of meeting up with her and Antonio. He did not feel comfortable enough to ask her out on her own at this stage. "You and your brother, I would like to meet with you sometime. What do you think? Would you want to do that?" he asked tentatively, not sure what response he would get.

"Why not?" replied Rosa. "That sounds like a nice idea. We know an exquisite place on Park Lane, at one of the best hotels; would you like to come for dinner with us tomorrow?"

"I certainly would, thank you, Rosa." Rosa could hear the smile in Alex's voice when he quickly accepted.

The next evening, Antonio and Rosa took a taxi into town at 6.30 PM, ready to meet their date at 7:00. Rosa was wearing her best dress, which was shimmering and glamorous, along with the beautiful topaz earrings, which Robert had given to Bella all those years ago, that matched her eyes. Her scent was sweet, and Antonio could not resist kissing her in the back of the taxi.

"Dear Rosa, any man would fall straight in love with you. I am so lucky. I am jealous that you will be spending this time with Alex," he said, smiling but half serious.

"Antonio, you are my one true love," she said, taking his hand between her soft, long fingers. "That will never change, you know that!"

Antonio rested his head on her shoulder. "I am the most handsome, I know that really!" Antonio joked.

As he arrived for dinner, Alex looked visibly impressed by the venue. There were huge chandeliers and gold-trimmed mirrors. He had never been anywhere so grand in his life.

The three of them sat down to dinner, and Antonio stayed quiet. Part of the reason for keeping silent was so that

Alex could devote his full attention to Rosa and be suitably wooed by her beauty and charisma.

They all ate three courses of delicious cuisine and drank wine. Then, at the end of the meal, Antonio was given a message by the waiter that he needed to go and attend to some business.

In actual fact, Jean and Clara had arranged this from their hotel so that Rosa and Alex could have more intimate time together. They stayed at the restaurant until closing time, talking and joking. Alex loved Rosa's company and kept looking dreamily into her eyes. Rosa did not feel the same and could not wait to return home to her beloved Antonio, but she played along with the game, firmly keeping the future in mind.

At the end of the evening, Alex walked Rosa to her taxi and kissed her hand. "What a wonderful evening, thank you, my dear Rosa. Can we do this again?"

She smiled and said, "Of course, we will speak soon. Good night, Alex." She shut the taxi door, and the car drove off while Alex watched her disappear into the distance.

Alex `s feelings towards Rosa were growing day by day. He constantly thought about Rosa's pretty face and started to believe she was the woman of his dreams. Over the coming months, he sent her flowers before their meetings and wrote her love notes. Not a day would go by without him lavishing attention on her in some way. He was smitten.

Meanwhile, after consultations with the two lovers, Clara and Jean had bought a very large store building with a basement in a quiet area. They also bought an empty house just opposite the store, and the two places were connected via an underground tunnel.

Using Rosa's civil engineering skills, they mapped out the store and how it should function to complete the next steps of the plan. They built several rooms at the top, on the side away from the road.

In the basement, there were four walls and a ceiling and floors made from hard and thick concrete. There were two air pipes on the ceiling, one taking polluted air out and the other bringing clean air in. Each pipe also has a fan inside it for ventilation.

They created a bedroom and lounge joined together and a small kitchen. On the right side of the kitchen there was a wardrobe, and on the left hand side of the kitchen, they built a bathroom. They also separated the lounge and the bedroom with a long wall from the main entrance.

The main entrance to the basement was made of two separate electrical steel doors, which were impossible to break, and the way they operated was crucial to the plan; they were watertight. One door let one enter a small space between the basement entrance and the main entrance to the rooms so that one would have one steel door in front one behind. But both doors would never be open at the same time. Inside the space, a note hanging from the wall read, "Once the second door opens, please enter immediately to avoid being intoxicated by the poisonous gas, which will automatically be released into this space within fifteen seconds of the second door opening."

When one passed the second door, there was another note on the wall next to it. The same message was written in thick black ink on various walls around the basement.

It took them several months to get the basement fit for its intended purpose. Each day that passed meant that Alex worshipped Rosa more. It was all going perfectly; the only person who was really unhappy with the developments between Alex and Rosa was Emma. She tried everything she could to turn Alex against Rosa, making up stories about her and trying to question her love for him. Sometimes she would call her names across the street, which hurt Rosa greatly.

Rosa felt awful that she was taking away Emma's love from her when she had no interest in Alex, and she was becoming increasingly tired of his advances. She was bored by having to spend so much time with him and longed to be with Antonio more. The situation was depressing her greatly, and she wished she could just give up the plan, but every time she talked to Antonio or Robert about this, she was encouraged to hang on a little longer in pursuit of a perfect future.

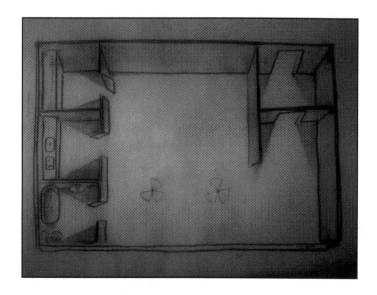

Clara and Jean also encouraged her to be patient and not to give up, reminding her that this was the most difficult step of the plan, but that life would be much easier once it was completed.

Rosa and Antonio were nearly thirty years old by now, and they had been in Britain for two years. Alex was feeling frustrated that Rosa kept delaying their future, never committing to being with him properly. She would talk about their future but would never agree to anything. He was becoming desperate and miserable.

One Sunday morning, Alex was taking a walk along the river by himself, pondering his future with Rosa. He felt like his head was going to explode with the pressure, and so he jumped in a taxi and headed for Rosa's home in Battersea. He knocked the door and Antonio answered, who stammered his best greeting. "Is Rosa home?"

Alex asked. Antonio nodded and ushered Alex into the lounge.

Rosa was upstairs doing her hair when she heard Alex's voice through the ceiling. She quickly finished her makeup and came downstairs. She saw Alex, his hair ruffled and his face tired. He hadn't shaved for two days. "Alex, what's wrong? Are you okay?"

"Not really, Rosa." He took a deep breath and replied, "I cannot sleep for thinking about you; you know how much I love you, don't you?"

She looked worried. "Yes, of course, but what is wrong?"

Alex knelt down on his knees with tears in his eyes. "I don't ever want to be without you, Rosa."

She knelt down and touched his face, even though it made her cold to do this in front of Antonio. "I feel the same Alex, but what can we do?"

I want to go to Italy, meet your father, and ask him for your hand in marriage. I cannot wait any longer, my darling. I need you."

Rosa felt relieved that the plan had worked and accepted immediately. "Oh, Alex, that is wonderful news. I will inform my father, and we will travel next week to see him. Of course I'll marry you."

She beamed at him, and Alex, still on his knees, put his head in her hands and breathed a huge sigh of relief. "You have made me so happy," he replied, crying more.

"Calm down my dear. I am as happy as you are, but I have to go. I will see you later."

Alex left with his heart and soul playing tunes of love inside his body. He ran through the park with elation, while

Rosa went back inside and shared the news to the team. They rejoiced knowing the next part of the plan, which would see Alex being introduced to everyone in Italy as Antonio's lookalike, would now take off.

Antonio was to go with them, but there was one major issue in that his friends would be expecting Antonio to talk normally. To get around this, Rosa revealed to Alex that Antonio had been undergoing intensive therapy to clear his stammer, and that as part of the therapy, he was to avoid talking for another two months.

At the same time, Robert made it known to locals that Antonio had throat problems and that he was not allowed to talk. Luckily, Alex couldn't speak Italian, and most of Robert's associates could not speak English; Alex was unlikely to reveal that he believed Antonio was overcoming a stutter, not that he has had throat problems.

The locals threw a big party for the return of their favourite siblings, the Agnolis,. They were also keen to meet Rosa's new love. Antonio, Rosa, and Alex were overwhelmed at the welcome they received when they arrived. The look on people's faces when they saw Antonio's lookalike was pure shock. They were astounded at the uncanny similarity. Robert of course was profoundly happy by the resemblance, and he shook Alex's hand vigorously. The group hugged for a long time shedding cups of tears between them at the emotional reunion. Antonio received many more hugs from locals wishing him well in his recovery, but he was desperate to talk and laugh with his father, even though he couldn't in public.

Robert spent the day taking Alex to meet all the important people in the family's life. Alex fell in love with the city and the people and took a long lunch with family friends, drinking lots of Robert's favourite wine and enjoying rich food and the best fruit. They then took a relaxing walk around the neighbourhood before bed. The locals were excited about Rosa's surprise engagement and wished them well, hoping for an invite to what they imagined would be a very grand wedding indeed.

Robert couldn't believe that his plan was finally coming together, and Alex was overjoyed at the respect and adoration he received because he was becoming part of such a loving family. A fantastic new world was opening to him – or so he thought.

Robert decided that the very next day there would be a wonderful engagement party for Alex and Rosa, and everyone should be there. Antonio felt even more despondent at this news, but he tried to remain positive. Robert called the local caterers to prepare Rosa's favourite food and drink. They would have the best exotic fruit, prime beef, and the freshest fish in abundance. He arranged the most magnificent marquee to go in his garden and had it filled with balloons, lights, and pretty decorations in Rosa's favourite colours. Alex felt very excited about the party, but Rosa felt a little sick at the thought of it. She took some pills to calm her nerves and get through the occasion so that she could try to make everyone believe she was in love with Alex.

The next day, Rosa awoke, had a long bath, and made herself feel beautiful before arriving at the party. Everyone was dressed in their most splendid attire for the event. The weather was perfect and Alex was glowing.

Meanwhile, Antonio didn't feel very comfortable being

at the party, and so he got closer to his father and whispered in his ear that he wanted to visit his friend in another city. Robert understood completely. Antonio held his father's hands and kissed them, and then he left, taking some car keys and a small bag.

When Rosa saw him leave, her heart sank and she ran after him. She wanted to tell him she loved him more than anything or anyone. But he had gone – the car sped off into the distance, and she was left with tears in her eyes. She was trying so hard to convince people she was in love with Alex, but all she thought about was Antonio.

Rosa wiped her tears and returned to the party to do her duty. Everyone was cheering her and Alex, toasting their love with the finest champagne. The party went on like this for two hours. People danced, laughed, and enjoyed a fantastic day. Then there was a telephone call for Robert; he was informed by a member of staff to come to the phone in the dining room.

Robert held the phone for a moment, his eyes blank, his face whiter than snow. Twenty seconds later, he dropped the phone and fell to a chair.

The phone call was about Antonio. He had been in a car accident; the car had overturned, and his body had been found burned in the car. For the second time in his life, Robert felt as though his insides had been torn from his soul. He let out an almighty wail of pain and fell to his knees.

Robert's servants were all screaming, and the party came to a halt. Rosa and Alex ran inside to Robert's side. He was slumped in the chair with tears streaming from his eyes. The news that came next made Rosa hysterical. An older servant took her hand. "My dear, it's Antonio – he has been found dead in the car. He had a terrible accident. I am truly sorry."

There was a stunned silence around the house and garden. Rosa could not breathe; she hyperventilated and convulsed as she fell on her knees, holding Robert's legs tightly.

Their worlds had been crushed; they had never in their wildest nightmares expected something like this. All of this work they'd all done, all these years – everything was torn apart. They had nothing left to live for; Antonio had been the centre of both their worlds.

Robert's mind was numb and raced about what on earth would happen to himself, Rosa, Alex, and the money. How would he live without his beloved boy, his only blood relation?

"I cannot go on," said Robert. "I don't want to live anymore; I do not want to take any more breaths on this earth if my only son is not here. Please tell me it's not true. I can't believe this, I don't want to believe it. It can't be real."

"Father, I want to die too. I don't want to live; I can't go on without him," sobbed Rosa. She turned to the staff member. "How can this be? It can't be, can it? Tell me it's a dream." She lied on the floor like a baby, in the foetal position and cradling herself, while Alex stroked her hair.

Soon after, the family's master servant ensured that both Robert and Rosa were taken to bed and given sedatives. They both had an assistant in their room at all times over the next few days, seeing to their needs. They hardly ate or slept, taking only sugar solution to retain some strength.

Antonio's body was returned in a coffin, and he was

buried immediately. Robert and Rosa were brought out of their house to see him buried, but they were too numb to speak, suffocated by the tragedy.

Crowds of people visited the home daily to bring flowers and pay their respects over the next few days. Everyone tried their best to comfort Rosa and Robert, but nothing worked; they were getting thinner and more withdrawn as the days went by.

Alex didn't know what to do to help. He himself was very sad about the tragic accident but could not console his new family. He asked for Robert's permission to return to Britain for a while.

The merchant's thoughts were jumbled and desperate. He looked at Alex with bloodshot eyes and said, "You are so like Antonio to me. It is like looking at him, and you joke like him. I want you to promise me that you will always take care of Rosa for me. She will need you more than ever now." Robert was not thinking clearly and hadn't properly considered that Rosa was not in love with Alex. He was just a desperate man who felt as though he had no options. For the last thirty years, he had been thinking about his plan for Antonio and his wealth, but that had all ended. He did not know where to turn. What was left?

"Of course, Father," Alex said, putting his hand comfortingly on Robert's shoulder. He then left Robert and went up to Rosa's room.

She did not flinch when he entered. She was crouched like a baby under her blankets. Alex rolled her towards him to look at her face. It was like death. His pretty Rosa had faded, with little food or drink for over a week. "My love, I am so worried about you, but I don't know what I can do. I need to go back to London for a while, but I will return soon to take care of you, I promise."

He stood there for a few moments, but Rosa did not respond. She had said nothing all week. "I will see you soon," he said, kissing her head before leaving. He left the same day.

That night, Clara and Jean, who'd found out Alex had gone back to Britain, arrived at the house and asked the servants to see Robert immediately. They went upstairs to find Rosa and Robert sitting in Antonio's room, hugging each other and crying.

When the Agnolis saw them, they were a little shocked. They had expected Clara and Jean to arrive much sooner to offer them support. But Rosa and Robert showed no outward reaction. Clara and Jean were disturbed to see the two of them so distraught. "We are so sorry we could not come before now," said Jean. "We—"

Robert interrupted them angrily. "Why on earth have you turned up here a week after my son has been buried? This is not what I expect from my friends." He got up and aimlessly shook his fist in the air, not knowing what to do with himself. "We do not know what to do with ourselves here. Our lives are over; we might as well both be dead ourselves," he screamed.

Jean looked terrified and tried to speak. "I know you were really distraught when you heard the news about your son, but—"

Robert interrupted again. "I have always forgiven you if it has been required, Jean, but you were responsible for my son!" he shouted while grabbing at the air .

Clara's eyes were full of tears as she watched Robert and Rosa's suffering. She grabbed his arm and said calmly, "Robert, listen to me – your son, Antonio, he is not dead; he is alive!"

Robert said, "I know my son is so great that he will always live on in our hearts and minds, but he is still gone. I will never see him again, and my limbs are numb. You two will have to sort my business for me now; I have been growing old, and now that Antonio is gone, I am too weak to work anymore. Please make sure everything is taken care of for me and Rosa." He fell to the floor with his head in his hands. Rosa cried like a baby every time her father mentioned Antonio's name, and she was constantly wiping her eyes.

Jean could not take any more of the pain. He stood up and shouted, "Robert! Listen to what I'm telling you. Please, sit down. Antonio is not dead. Can you hear me? Do you understand? He is alive. This is the next part of the plan completed, but different to how you expected. It works very well this way, though."

Robert threw his arms into the air and raged, "What plan? Explain quickly!"

Jean spoke quietly. "Antonio really is not dead, I promise you. We saw that the only way people would believe Antonio was dead was if they saw him buried in front of their own eyes. Do you see?"

Robert stopped Jean and screamed, "Was it a plan to kill my son? What on earth are you talking about? Are you crazy?"

Then Rosa grabbed Clara's arm angrily. "Tell me the

truth! What the hell have you been doing without telling us? I don't understand this."

Everyone was shouting across the room, hysterically trying to sort out the confusion. Jean turned to Robert and said loudly, "Look, we didn't tell you about this because we wanted it to look completely realistic when you and Rosa were mourning for Antonio. We needed your sadness to look genuine. Do you see?"

Robert stopped and dropped his hands to his sides and looked down. He did not know what to believe at this moment in time. His head hurt and his brain ached.

Clara held Rosa tightly to stop her body from shaking, and she stroked her hair. "I am so terribly sorry. We thought it was the best way for people to believe that Antonio was gone."

At this point, Robert became delirious, hopping around the room laughing and crying at the same time. He was acting like he was insane. "Oh my god, Antonio is not dead. My son, my beloved son! Oh my god, oh my god. I am the happiest man alive. Thank you, God!"

Rosa held tightly on to Clara. "This is the best news I will ever have in my life. My Antonio, my Antonio!" She danced with Clara around the room, and they all laughed together, happily celebrating and trying to forget the pain and suffering.

That evening they talked for hours and rejoiced happily that Antonio was fine; their plan was back on course. They stayed up all night chatting about everything. Meanwhile Antonio was safe back in London, hiding in the store, away from everyone and ready to continue with the next part of the plan.

In the morning, Rosa took a short nap and then got ready to go back to London. She was beyond tired but was bursting at the thought of seeing her Antonio once more. She had to keep reminding herself that everything was okay again. Clara and Jean also came back to London with her, after another emotional good-bye with Robert. He was sad at being left alone again but hoped to see his boy soon, and this thought kept him going.

As soon as Rosa arrived, she took a taxi straight to the store. She could hardly breathe at the thought of seeing Antonio again. When the car pulled up outside, she leapt out with her stuff and threw some money at the driver, almost ripping her jacket in the door. When she saw him, her heart melted again and she kissed him all over. His head, his eyes, his ears, his mouth – she could not believe she was seeing him again in the flesh. She loved him so much she wanted to consume him, for their bodies to be as one. Antonio had tears in his eyes and held her tight, not wanting to let her go. He had been stuck in the store alone for days and felt a little miserable and lonely. Seeing Rosa elevated his spirits so much.

Now the next part of the plan could begin. The next day, Rosa informed Alex that she had returned but that she was still deeply devastated about Antonio and wanted to be alone. This was a good excuse for her to only see Alex once or twice a week. She preferred to spend as little time with him as possible so that she could be with her real love.

Alex was overjoyed to see his fiancée looking better. He

wanted to wrap her up in love and take care of her, but he knew she wanted to spend time alone, and he wanted to respect her wishes. He stayed away as much as possible, even though it upset him to be alone. He told her, she should call him if she needed anything.

Meanwhile Clara and Jean were doing everything they could to make the next part of the plan run more smoothly for the Agnolis. They were working non-stop on all the finer details, including creating a wig for Antonio which matched Alex's hair, based on a photo taken at the engagement party. Physically there were no other changes to be made because they were so identical.

They also bought a video camera for Rosa to record Alex every time she saw him. She told him that she wanted to have memories of him forever, and also that it comforted her father to see the films because they reminded him so much of Antonio. Alex was led to believe that Robert had bought them the expensive video camera as an engagement present and that Rosa wanted to learn how to use it properly by practising on Alex. Meanwhile, Antonio was being fully trained in bank management so that he could do Alex's job perfectly.

After spending some time looking through the networks for a bright but ordinary person who was an expert in bank management, the group found someone called David. He was a forty-five-year-old Londoner who was quiet and kept himself to himself. He didn't have a family and wasn't especially sociable, but he was a good teacher. He came to the house opposite the store four days a week, for six hours each day, to teach Antonio all the essentials of bank management:

the day-to-day running of the bank, what was expected of the manager, how could excel in his job and always keep customers and bosses happy, and so on. Antonio was picking it up well, and because he was in the store alone all the time, he had plenty of hours to revise and study. Rosa lived in her house in Battersea on her own, but she would go to see Antonio late most evenings, and if she'd filmed Alex in the day, she would take him the footage to watch. In between training in banking skills, Antonio would learn how to copy Alex's voice and mannerisms, and also how he interacted with other people.

Alex didn't mind being filmed, but he was finding it difficult being constantly made aware by Rosa that he was not allowed to kiss or touch her beautiful skin. Rosa had told him that in her culture the bride and groom were not allowed to be intimate with each other until their wedding day. And, even if that was not the case, she was too upset about Antonio to want to be intimate with anyone for the time being. Alex felt angry and frustrated deep down, but he tried his best to keep calm because he did not want to upset Rosa. He wanted to stick to the traditions of her noble family and not offend them with his lust.

Behind the scenes, Clara and Jean were surreptitiously gathering information about Alex's life. They captured photos of him with his friends, found out more about who they were, and noted how he acted with them. It was a detailed job which required a high level of intellect, but they both had very good minds and collected some vital information for the plan. Rosa was providing essential information and details whenever possible.

Six months of training and information gathering passed. There was so much to be done. Antonio was picking everything up, but he still had more to learn to complete the task absolutely faultlessly. He did not want to let everyone down because they were all working so hard on the plan.

Alex was struggling with the situation and one day found the courage to speak to Rosa again about his feelings. "Rosa, my dear, when do you think you will be ready for us to marry? I am finding it so difficult to wait for such a long time, and it is painful. I need to be close to you."

She looked scornfully at him. "Alex, don't be so inconsiderate. In our family community in Italy, if a close relative is lost, there must be no parties or celebrations for at least a year. I thought you understood this."

He looked at the floor, like a dog that had been disobedient. "Yes, sorry, Rosa. I will not mention it again."

While all of this was happening, Emma was still desperately trying to find out more about Rosa in the hopes of turning Alex against her. She continued to try everything she could to make Alex stop loving Rosa, but nothing would work.

Whenever Rosa and Alex met up, Rosa always made sure that she left his company by 7:00 PM so that she could return to Antonio at the store. Alex sometimes insisted on her staying a little later with him, but as soon as she could, she would take a taxi back to the store.

On one particular evening, Alex was feeling amorous and invited Rosa for a one-off late dinner. She did not want to accept but felt obliged to, because she had not spent much time with him recently. At work during the day, he told everyone how excited he was to be having dinner with his fiancée. He didn't stop smiling, which was a rare occasion for him. Emma of course was incensed by Alex's upbeat mood and was angry that Rosa would be enjoying him while she was home alone. She often sat in her little flat dreaming about her manager. Tonight she decided she would give Rosa a piece of her mind. What was the point of Rosa being with Alex anyway, when she did not want to spend time with him and show him the love that Emma could? Emma sensed that Alex was being misguided, and this gave her hope to one day be with him.

That night Emma waited in secret in an alley near Rosa's home, after finding her address on the bank's system. It was about 11.30 PM when she heard the tyres of a taxi pull up and what sounded like Alex's voice in the distance. Rosa got out, said goodnight, and shut the door. The taxi waited for her to let herself into the house and then drove off. Emma silently watched for a minute, and as soon as the taxi had driven away, she saw Rosa come out of the house wearing a long coat and covering her head with a big black scarf. She wondered what on earth Rosa was doing this late at night. Rosa started walking quickly through the streets, checking that no one was following her, while Emma hung back in the distance, staying hidden. She became more and more curious about what was going on. Five minutes later, Rosa had arrived in a quiet and deserted area not far from the store. She looked around again to check she was safe and then continued. The night was so black, with hardly any moon and poor street lighting, and so Emma could not be seen despite Rosa's efforts.

Antonio was in the house opposite the store as always, waiting for Rosa. He was always worried that one day someone might follow her, but Rosa told him he was being silly. He looked through a gap in the curtains and could see Rosa coming up the street – and he was sure that he could see a small figure in the distance behind her. Then the figure would disappear, and he wondered if he'd imagined it –before he would see something flicker again. Antonio's heart was racing now, pulsating in his chest. His instant reaction was to grab his hand gun from the wardrobe and run through the underground passageway to the store, and waited behind the door, trying to stop his heavy breathing. He was hot and sweating with the stress.

Rosa opened the door first, and Antonio grabbed her forcefully from behind and pulled her into the darkness of the room. She gasped, and Antonio whispered in her ear, "It's me, Antonio. Don't scream."

Rosa relaxed a little when she heard Antonio's voice, but her heart was pounding. She was terrified and still hadn't closed the door behind her. Antonio then waited silently for Emma.

She arrived at the door hardly making a sound, and she quietly pushed the door, entering very slowly. She then felt Antonio's large hand wrap itself around her mouth as he pulled her towards him. She yelped, and he put his gun to her head. He whispered to her, "If you move, I will kill you." Emma wrestled with him and tried to free herself. Her muffled cries were becoming increasingly louder. Antonio panicked. "Shush, stop moving or I will kill you. I mean it."

Emma was shaking; she had never been so petrified in

all her life. Why did she follow someone into a dark house? She stayed as still as possible, but her hands kept shaking a little.

Antonio whispered into her ear, "Who is with you? Why are you following Rosa? Emma tried to answer, but Antonio was still covering her mouth. He released his grip a little and said again, "If you scream, I will kill you."

Emma nodded her head tearfully and begged, "For God's sake, please don't kill me. I am just on my own, I promise." At this point, Antonio pushed her away and quickly looked outside to check there was no one else around. He closed the door immediately and grabbed Emma again.

Antonio was now wearing the wig so that his hair would look the same as Alex's. As Emma got closer to him, she looked horrified. "Is that you, Alex? Alex?" she said, her voice trembling.

Antonio put the gun to her head again. "What do you want? Why are you following Rosa?" he said, both screaming and whispering at the same time. Emma was fully aware that Alex had an extreme temper when he was annoyed, and so she knew that her following Rosa was likely to make him furious. She wasn't sure of exactly what he was capable of. Would he really kill her? "Alex, I am pleading with you, don't kill me."

He grabbed her tighter. "Shush. Just tell me who has sent you!"

At this point, Rosa came out from the darkness, and Emma went crazy, shouting abuse at her. "You bitch, you whore! What have you turned Alex into?"

"Shut up!" raged Antonio. "If one more word comes out of your mouth, you will be dead.

"But, Alex, it's me, Emma – do you not recognise me? What's happened to you? What is this gun? Surely you wouldn't kill me? It is ridiculous." Emma foolishly was still trying to charm who she thought was Alex, pouting her lips at him.

"Do not get any closer, I'm warning you," he spoke slowly but firmly. "Tell me why you are following Rosa."

Emma broke down, crying hysterically. "Alex, I was following Rosa because I thought she was up to something, and I was trying to protect you. Do you see? Please forgive me. I should have stayed away, but I am so in love with you. I was desperate." Emma stood back, half expecting that Antonio would shoot her there and then. He looked so mad, and was sweating profusely.

Antonio played along and let Emma believe he was Alex. He was grinding his teeth together and was deeply distraught at the situation they'd all found themselves in. He didn't know what to do. "Emma, Emma, what have you done. Why for God's sake did you need to follow Rosa for me?"

Her voice became even more weak and needy. "Alex, I will never make a mistake like this ever again, I promise you. I don't know what I was thinking. I just love you so much; I wanted to be with you. You are all I ever think about – you are my world."

Rosa stood in the dark, still silent. She was distraught at the situation and felt deeply sad that Emma was in danger just because she was in love with Alex. At this moment she wished she'd never been involved in this plan; she craved a normal life like she saw other people having.

In a blind panic, Antonio lashed out and hit Emma over

the head with his gun. He hit her so hard she immediately lost consciousness and fell to the floor with a crash.

Rosa screamed at him angrily and tearfully, "What the hell did you do that for?" She rushed to Emma and tried to wake her up, but she wasn't moving.

Antonio looked at her guiltily and replied, "I didn't know what else to do."

Rosa touched Emma's head and looked up at Antonio. "Well, what are we going to do with her now?" Both of them knew that they could not let her go because it would mean the end of years of planning on their part, not to mention all the work Clara and Jean had done. And most important, they didn't want to destroy their father's dream. They lifted Emma together and dragged her body to the basement. There was no way they could kill her because Robert would not agree to such a thing.

They would have to leave her there for the time being while they quickly finished the plan. They locked the door and immediately called Clara and Jean.

At this point, inside the basement, a drowsy Emma was regaining consciousness. She felt dizzy, her head was heavy and painful, and her blond hair was drenched in sweat. She looked around the dark room, confused. As her eyes adjusted, she could see she was in a very strange place but didn't know where it was or what she was doing there. She spotted the door and pushed herself up to try to open it, but it wouldn't move. Emma automatically screamed and screamed. She was frantic, hysterical. Her memory was fuzzy, and she had no idea what was going on. She began to cry again, hopelessly.

It was at that moment she looked up and saw a large notice written on the wall in thick black ink. It read:

1. You are in a prison. If you want to live, follow the instructions below.

Her eyesight was fuzzy, but she strained and kept reading. The notice continued.

When the door opens, look at what is waiting and take whatever you want or need. There will be all your daily essentials.
2. If you step out of the door into the space between this door and the second door, ensure you come back within fifteen mint, otherwise this door will lock and you will be stuck in this space with a poisonous gas for five days.
3. If the second door opens, do not try to stop it closing as this will cause the poisonous gas to escape, and you will die within seconds.
4. If you are not present when the door opens for your essentials, then you will have to wait until the following day.
I hope you will follow these instructions. Good luck.

Emma's mind collapsed when she read this. She read it again and again, thinking she must be dreaming. She screamed her head off, kicking and punching the walls at the same time. "Alex, please rescue me. Alex!" But there was no way anyone could possibly hear her; it was useless. She almost passed out with hysteria, but then she saw another sign in black writing on the other wall in the same writing. It read, "Do not think about Rosa. Either you accept that you have been imprisoned ,or you commit suicide and free yourself from living underground. There are no other options."

Emma saw it and imagined that Alex had wrote it and done this to her so she could never harass Rosa ever again. This way, the two could happily be together without Emma bothering them and she either had to kill herself or resign herself to living with rats and mice for the rest of her life. She couldn't believe this was really happening.

She screamed again and again, but no reply ever came. She looked around her and saw the kitchen; she ran to it to see her surroundings and above the sink was another notice. It read, "Requirements for Suicide and Requirements for Survival."

She continued screaming, making herself sick. She ran to the next room and found a small bathroom with a mirror hanging on the wall opposite the bathroom door entrance.

She saw herself in the mirror and noticed the white bandage wrapped around her head, and slowly the incident with the gun came flooding back into her mind.

She felt so weak and helpless that she could not even stand on her feet. She sat down in the corner of the room and wrote down the time and date: "2.40 AM, 02-08-1974." There she was, helpless and crying like a little girl in an underground cave, where no one could see or hear her. In her mind Alex had carried out this barbaric act because of another woman.

This hurt Emma so much because she had loved this man for so long.

In the outside world, Rosa, Antonio, and their two assistants continued work on the plan for a day or two. They knew that Emma's friends and family would wonder where she was, but they prayed people would just think she'd decided to go away for a while. They threw themselves into their work, trying to take their minds off what they had done to this innocent woman who had done nothing wrong, except get caught up in their plans. After a particularly intense day of organisation, Rosa and Antonio sat down with a glass of wine at the house opposite the store and switched on the TV. They chatted as the news reports in the background ran through the day's political events. There were stories about the queen, politicians, and actors whirling around them, but they were both so exhausted they didn't take in any of it.

After several minutes, a picture flashed up on screen that caught the corner of Antonio's eye, and he dropped his wine. The crimson liquid sprayed the carpet like a burst wound, and he put his hands through his hair despairingly while staring at Rosa. "God. Oh, God, Rosa," he whispered.

She sat next to him and put his head into the warmth of his neck. "I know," she said quietly. Neither of them knew what to say; their stomachs panged with the guilt. All that kept them going was each other and the thought of making their father contented.

The police and Emma's friends and family had searched for several days, combing the area for clues about her disappearance. On screen, a woman looking like an older version of Emma stood outside Emma's house. She was sobbing and looked like she hadn't slept for several days. "If anyone has any idea about where Emma might be, any idea whatsoever, I am pleading with you, let us know. We are so worried, the family is devastated. We will do anything to get her back." She broke down and was comforted by two older men while the camera moved away to show more photos of Emma.

The two lovers sat in silence for the rest of the evening, stroking each other's hands to pacify one another. They felt too sick to eat, and Rosa went home about 9.30 PM, on her own, feeling lost.

In the basement, Emma knew nothing about her distraught friends and family and just sat in heap, recording the days as they crawled by, each one feeling like it lasted a week. Minutes felt like hours and hours felt like days. She slept and slept some more and then lay awake staring at the ceiling for vast stretches of time.

A week after Emma's disappearance, two policemen came to the bank where Alex was working and asked to see him. They were ushered into his room, where he sat looking morose. He may have not loved Emma and even found her irritating, but he was still concerned. Everyone at the bank had been very quiet and sullen throughout the week. "Excuse me, sir, can we interrupt for a moment?" asked one of the policemen, opening Alex's office door. They were lofty and imposing, with stern expressions cast over their faces. One had his hat low down over his eyes.

Alex looked up. "Come in, sit down." He pointed to the chairs. "Is there news about Emma?"

"No, sir. We have come to find out more about your relationship with the girl," said the older of the two.

"What relationship?" Alex looked confused. "There was no relationship! What do you mean?"

"We hear that the lady had something of an …" The officer paused. "Infatuation with you?"

"Well yes, she wanted me to be her boyfriend. She always showed a lot of interest, but she knew I wasn't keen on her in that way."

"You were quite vexed by her advances, is that right?"

Alex didn't like the tone of the officer; he found it a little accusatory. "What are you saying?" he said, raising his voice.

"Calm down, Mr James," said the younger one, almost whispering. "We're not saying anything. We're just conducting our inquiries, building up a picture of Emma's relationship with her friends, family, and colleagues."

"Well, she wanted me and I didn't want her, that is all; you can spend your time more usefully somewhere else," he brushed them off.

"Mr James, we would like you to come to the station this afternoon to help with our investigation. It is quite routine in these matters," said the older officer, putting his notes back into his brief case.

"Officer, I'm a very busy man. I am working," Alex's retorted; his voice was starting to rise, and he had fury in his eyes.

"I'm sorry, sir, this is a requirement. Please come to the station at two o'clock. Thank you." With that both police officers nodded at Alex and left the room.

He kicked the chair. Not only was Emma's disappearance disrupting work at the bank, but he was now going to have to spend the whole afternoon at the police station and fall behind on his work. Alex was fuming.

As the weeks went by, hope of finding Emma diminished. The local papers mentioned her less and less, TV reports died down, and Rosa and Antonio got back into their everyday lives. They were deeply in love and wanted to be together all day and night, like two devoted young lovers. This encouraged them to work tirelessly to do everything that needed to be done. Antonio felt depressed that he and Rosa could not yet skip around the park together on a sunny day, or sit by the lake and feed the ducks. He longed for a time when this could happen – and the time had almost come. It had taken him a year of training, but he was now fully ready for the next step of the plan to happen.

Emma would think daily about how someone could do something like this to her. She hated Alex for the prison she believed he'd created, but she also missed him, and her heart was ripped apart in so many ways. She was tortured by the belief that Rosa and Alex were now free to be profoundly in love, and she was able to do nothing about it. How powerful must their feelings have been for each other that they would do something like this to be together, she thought.

Alex had asked Rosa about the wedding perhaps one hundred times, only to be brushed off and told he had to wait. It had been more than a year since their engagement, yet he was forced to stay away from her perfect lips to uphold Rosa and her family's traditions. But now, with Clara and Jean certain that Antonio was ready for the fifth and last step of the plan, a date could be set for the wedding.

At 10.00 AM on Monday, 4 February 1975, Rosa, who

had spent much time doing her hair and makeup, went into town feeling optimistic that things were moving forward. She walked over to the bank and made her way straight to Alex's office, where she had first met him. She opened his door, and Alex looked up startled. "Rosa! What is wrong?" He looked serious. Alex wasn't used to seeing his love at the bank; she never visited him there.

"Nothing is wrong!" she said with a smile. "Everything is good. I just want to talk to you." Rosa was sure to act as though she truly loved him.

"Of course, my dear," said Alex, standing up, holding her shoulders in his hands, and looking into her eyes. "What do you want to say?"

"Well, Alex, I know you have waited a long time to be with me properly – you've been very patient."

A smile swept across his face, and he touched her cheeks with his hands. "Say it, Rosa! Say what you want to say." He sounded like an excited schoolboy.

"You know I love you. I want to organise our wedding as soon as possible. I don't want us to wait any longer for this. Let's do it!" Rosa was very emotional for several reasons, but not because she loved Alex. However it was useful that she felt this way because it served to make Alex believe she was in love with him.

Alex's heart was racing and pounding; he had never felt so ecstatic before in his life. He hugged Rosa and lifted her off the ground. "Thank you, Rosa!" he shouted. "I love you so much! We will be so happy, I promise."

He twirled her around his desk, and by this point, the whole of the bank was wondering what the commotion was. Alex opened the door and shouted loudly, "Rosa and I are going to have our wedding this Friday. You are all invited!" Then he picked all the papers up from his desk and threw them in the air hysterically.

He jumped around the room and shouted, "I cannot believe it, we are getting married!"

With Alex`s so lively, all the bank staff immediately gathered and started joining in, clapping for the two of them. Some may not have liked him, but they felt they should show some happiness at the news. "I am giving you all the day of Friday; we will close the bank," he said with gusto.

The staff were dumbfounded. It was extremely rare for Alex to give people days off so freely. They chatted amongst themselves, finding this new good nature a shock.

With so few days to plan the wedding, Alex got to work straight away on making arrangements. There were so many things to do to make sure everything went according to plan, and he spent the next two days making hundreds of phone calls and visiting people. He organised the most exquisite cake, made from the finest fruit and liquors; he ordered the rarest, sweetest smelling flowers, including roses of course. He booked a spectacular band that would play romantic music for his bride and during a beautiful five-course Wedding breakfast, with the richest local foods. It was so important for him to make sure Rosa had the best day of her life.

Rosa spent some time choosing a wedding dress. It was whiter than the purest snow, with wonderful diamond detail around the waist band. She arranged for someone to do her hair and makeup, as well as a massage, pedicure, and manicure, and she booked a photographer.

They chose pink and purple, Rosa's favourite colours, as the colour scheme and invited as many people as they could on such short notice. For many people, particularly those in Italy, it was very short notice and several could not make it, but they would still have more than enough guests. Robert was invited to present his only daughter to her husband on the special day.

As the hours ticked away, the two became increasingly excited – though for different reasons – but together they looked like any other happy couple.

Emma would not be at the wedding, of course, and she would have been distraught to have known about it. In her mind, Alex was hers and nobody else's , despite the fact she thought she'd never see him again.

On 7 February 1975, Emma awoke and wrote the date in the usual place as usual. She didn't know that this day, a wedding day, would mark a turbulent new chapter in all their lives.

It was an important day for Robert's plan. The merchant had always dreamed of seeing this day before he died, and now his wish was about to become reality.

Groups of guests started to make their way to the party, feeling happy and tingling with excitement about the impending event.

There were over two hundred people, dressed in lavish and exquisite outfits with hats, cummerbunds, glistening shoes, and grand dresses. There was frivolity in the air.

Rosa had told Alex that she wanted them both to look

perfect for their big day and that she had booked them into a local beauty salon to make sure their skin, hair, and clothes were absolutely right for their guests, for their photos, and of course for each other.

Alex had taken some persuading that he needed to go to have his hair professionally washed and styled, but he would do anything to keep his Rosa happy. His friends had joked with him that he gave in to Rosa too much, but he didn't care what anyone said; she was the only thing that mattered to him. She mattered even more because he hadn't been in touch with his own family since his troublesome teenage years, and now he was going to have his own family.

When they arrived at the salon, they were given five-star treatment. They both sat nervously in luxurious surroundings, drinking glasses of pink champagne and sinking into the huge silk sofas. But they were on edge for very different reasons. Rosa's palms were starting to sweat, and she didn't know how much longer she could keep up the pretence with Alex and everyone else.

She disappeared for a moment while Alex waited. His hands were now wet with sweat, and his heart beat quickly. Alex didn't like sitting there on his own without Rosa, and his mind kept thinking over his speech and whether he would saying everything right. Would he remember to thank everyone who needed to be thanked? He was paranoid about making a fool of himself in front of Rosa and the guests.

He stood up and started practising his speech, but Rosa quickly returned with a wide smile. "I have a gift for you, darling," she said, handing him a very handsome black suit. It was woven with the finest silks and linen and looked exactly his size. "I really hope you like it, my love," she said convincingly.

The groom wasted no time in taking the wrapper off. "Wow, it is amazing, Rosa. I am very grateful. This is so thoughtful; I am so lucky to have you." He smiled and kissed her cheeks twice and then her forehead and hands. "I am so nervous and excited about today. I can't wait to put this on," he said beaming.

"You will get to wear it soon, sweetheart, but we need to get our hair and makeup done first." Rosa then led Alex to a private room. It was quite small and had just one chair and a few bits of equipment.

Clara and Jean were dressed up as beauticians and waiting for him. "Please, sir, take a seat," said Jean to Alex. "Sit opposite the mirror in this chair, so I can do your face."

The chair was black leather and looked like a dentist's chair. Alex was upbeat. With a spring in his step, he got in the chair and smiled at the beautician. Jean pressed a lever on the bottom of the seat with his foot, and the chair moved upwards so Alex was in easy reach of him.

"What a great day! I bet you had your great day many, many years ago, old man," Alex joked, trying to lighten the tense atmosphere.

Jean took a small, black hand-towel and smiled. "Yes, I was looking forward to it so much, just like you. Although things don't always work out how you want them to, unfortunately."

As he said that, Jean clenched his teeth and put the towel, soaked with chloroform, over Alex's nose and mouth and held it there firmly.

Alex struggled for a few short seconds and then lost

consciousness. They all looked at each other. Rosa's heart was racing; she felt scared.

Jean lowered the chair with his foot and then picked Alex up under his arms, from behind. Clara and Rosa took a leg each, their eyes wide and flitting between the doorway and Alex's face.

They carefully eased him into a large, black body bag with holes in it to allow him to breathe, and they dragged his body out of the back door and straight into the boot of their car, parked right outside.

Rosa quickly called Antonio when Jean and Clara left, and she stayed there while Jean and Clara drove Alex to the store. They drove a little more slowly than usual so that they didn't attract any attention from the police or other drivers. They cautiously avoided pot holes or bumps in the road because they didn't want to jolt Alex around too much.

Antonio was bored and nervous and couldn't wait to get out. When he received the call from Rosa, he went to meet her at another real beauty salon nearby to properly get their hair and makeup done.

Rosa had hurried across town and felt a bit sick in the pit of her stomach, but she was relieved to see Antonio and receive a warm hug from him.

At the salon, they drank champagne with other brides and grooms and toasted each other. After a couple of glasses, they became more relaxed and enjoyed the process of being pampered at a five-star salon. Antonio got his beard trimmed and shaped and felt more dashing than he had in ages. He couldn't believe he was free; it was a truly mind-blowing feeling for him. Part of him had forgotten how to act with people. He knew it would take some adjustment to be in the real world again, particularly with a new identity.

They chatted to other couples about their lives and loves and enjoyed hearing the stories, although they had to be reserved about their own lives. They tried hard to be friendly without revealing any details; it was a taste of how things would be in their new lives. At least for a good while.

After two hours of grooming and with near perfect skin and hair, the lovers were driven in a beautiful white sports car to the wedding – a wedding that was mainly organised by Alex, but they had to forget that for today. They put Alex out of their minds and immersed themselves in the moment and in the whole occasion.

When they arrived, the guests assumed Antonio was Alex, as had been planned, and much cheering and clapping ensued. Guests threw money and confetti over the bride and the groom and were thoroughly convinced by Antonio's portrayal of Alex. "How am I doing?" he whispered to Rosa, sounding self-conscious.

"You are doing marvellously, my love, please don't worry; it will be fine. Everyone will be nice to us today because they want to see us happy," she reassured him.

It felt a little strange for Antonio to be the groom without being involved in any of the preparations. Rosa had explained everything that would be happening to him and how Alex had arranged everything, so that he could confidently talk about the preparations without arousing any suspicion.

He had hardly socialised with anyone for a year, but nevertheless he enjoyed himself and got into the role of the groom, focusing on his life with Rosa.

Rosa and Antonio felt like queen and king for the day, revelling in the love and warmth they received from all the guests. They savoured each wonderful moment, as did Robert, who hadn't see his son for so long. His heart longed to hug his son after so much time, but the merchant stayed quietly in the background and savoured seeing the two of them glowing together, so happy and so in love. His vision had become reality. He wanted to rush over to Antonio and put his arms around him, but he was self-conscious and thought it was better to wait until people were distracted by drinking and dancing, so the focus was not so strongly on the groom. He needed time to talk to him properly in private, to share what had been happening and discuss the future.

Antonio was chatting with Alex's friends and other guests, gleefully, and then suddenly saw Robert, looking still in the corner of the room. He stopped, his face looking serious. He was struck with emotion at seeing his devoted father after so many months. Antonio tried to remain calm so that he wasn't acting out of character, but he could not control his emotions and gave in. He went over to Robert and flung his arms around him, his eyes welling up. "It is so good to see you, my dear father. I have missed you so very much."

When people saw this scene, there were lots of smiles and encouragement. Everyone thought Alex, Robert's son-in-law, was overcome with emotion at marrying his daughter. It was, after all, very respectful to show love to your father-in-law in Italian culture.

The crowd raised their glasses, and Rosa also ran to Robert to embrace him, crying at the same time. Robert kept calm as possible and patted the two children's hair and faces proudly as they all held each other.

The crowds had their champagne glasses topped off, and the air rippled with chiming and clinking glasses as they toasted the family.

At four o'clock, the couple and their party walked next door to a glorious eighteenth-century church. Its ceilings depicted the gods and was decorated in ornate gold. The seats and fittings were made from heavy, dark timber ,and the mesmerising stained glass windows let in multicoloured hues of exuberant light.

Once everyone was in place, Robert walked Rosa gracefully down the aisle as a violinist and harpist played "The Wedding March". The air was expectant, and Robert held his head high, nodding at guests proudly as he and Rosa walked past them. It was a long walk, and Rosa's ample dress cascaded wildly behind her like armfuls of rich, pearly ribbon. Her two flower girls, Isabella and Rosanna, aged five and seven, smiled angelically at everyone as they tried to hold the back of the bride's dress for her.

They arrived in front of the altar, and Antonio thanked his father, took Rosa's hand, and gazed at her through her veil with the eyes of a devoted puppy.

The minister rose to address them. "Dearly beloved, we are gathered here today to witness the marriage vows of Alex and Rosa, a couple who have been deeply in love for a number of years and now wish to have God's blessing for their partnership. I will ask you now, if any persons present know a reason why this couple should not be joined together in holy matrimony, please speak now."

He was silent for a few minutes while the room stays quiet. All that can be heard were a few coughs. The couple flicked each other a quick glance and then looked back at the altar. They both breathed a sigh of relief when the minister began talking again.

"Alex David White, do you take Rosa Bella Agnoli to be your lawful wife? To have and to hold her in sickness and in health, for richer, for poorer from this day forward?" said the minister.

"I do," says Antonio, coughing afterwards. In his head, he quickly said, "God, forgive me" before giving a sweeping look up towards the heavens.

"Will you love and cherish her, respect her and honour her?" asked the minister.

"I will," Antonio replied, looking and smiling at Rosa.

Rosa then went through her vows, speaking quietly but faultlessly, and afterwards Antonio was allowed to lift the veil and kiss the bride before the congregation. They held each other's faces in their hands and grinned like excited children. Then they both turned, and Antonio lead Rosa back down the aisle, stopping every few seconds as they posed for photographs.

Outside of the church, the photographer rounded up different groups of friends and family to take pictures for the wedding album, and the waiting staff offered everyone pink champagne. Plates of cream cheese rolled in smoked salmon arrived, followed by mini chocolate and raspberry puddings. Rosa and Antonio began to relax in the tranquil, green surroundings. Then, half an hour later, they walked back to Robert's house to continue the party.

Clara and Jean were on the other side of town, waiting for Alex to partly regain his consciousness so that they could put him in the underground. Emma had no idea that she was about to be joined by the love of her life or that the outside world was enjoying so much frivolity today.

The party was alive and electric. Alex, on the other hand, might as well have been dead. The day he had waited so long for had been ripped from beneath him, and it was unlikely he would ever see his bride again.

As he started to wake up, Clara and Jean carried him down to the underground and left him there. He had been heavy and awkward to carry, and their backs were sore. They quickly exited the underground before he woke up fully.

Emma darted towards the door, thinking her monthly delivery of food and essentials had arrived. She stopped in her tracks and gasped when she saw Alex lying there in a heap.

Emma was livid beyond belief. She threw herself at him and started kicking and punching him angrily. "You son of a bitch! Why the hell have you put me through this, imprisoned me like this?" she wailed. "I have been here for so long, without anyone. I have been treated like a dog. What are you doing to me? Why do you think you can do this, you pig? You are the most disgusting, sick person I've ever met. You are pure evil." Emma was wearing herself out with her tirade, but she kept on and on.

Alex's eyes were fuzzy with the anaesthetic, and Emma could not see through her clearly temper. He looked up at her and took a few moments to focus as she continued to kick him in the legs, jolting his whole body and making him feel sick.

Her face became clearer, but his mind was still very blurred. Alex mustered up all his strength to speak. "Emma? Is that Emma? What is going on, what are you doing here? Jesus, what the hell is happening?" His body was listless. He slumped again, gently muttering, "I thought you were dead." He drifted in and out of consciousness.

Emma's eyes were red with rage. "You want me dead, eh? You bastard! You wanted to get rid of me, huh? Who the hell do you think you are taking people's lives into your own hands? My friends and my family, what do they think has happened to me? They must be mortified. How can you do this?"

Alex slowly came around, rubbing his eyes and shaking his body and trying to understand what was going on. He tried to shield himself from Emma. "Why are you hiding here, Emma? Where are we?" His mind was swirling with all sorts of thoughts. He was gradually starting to recall that something bad had happened, but he wasn't sure what; he just thought Emma had something to do with it. He thought she'd hatched a plan to keep him away from Rosa so that she could be with him.

Alex stood up and looked at Emma like he always used to, with hate in his eyes. "Why have you put me here? You haven't done anything to Rosa, have you? If you touch Rosa, I won't be responsible for my actions. You prostitute! What have you done? Let me out of here."

"Don't you talk to me about that prostitute Rosa! You

put me in here to keep me away from that bitch. What the hell do you think you're doing?" she screamed in his face.

"Where is my Rosa? You evil woman, what have you done with her?" he raged, grabbing her throat with his hand, intent on suffocating her. He'd never liked her, and now his disdain for Emma knew no bounds.

Emma's face turned blue; she was weak and couldn't breathe. Alex was tightening his grip violently. As he did so, he looked up saw the writing on the wall, which read, "Don't think about Rosa. You either accept that you have been imprisoned or you commit suicide and free yourself from living."

He automatically dropped his hand and walked closer to the wall, staring intensely at the words. His eyes fixated on the message.

Emma started breathing again; she coughed a little and then cried hopelessly. "Please, leave me alone, Alex," she begged. "Do you really want to kill me?"

Alex was stunned at the words on the wall; his throat was as dry as sandpaper. He was convinced Emma had been completely devious and had done some awful deeds – but Emma thought Alex had written the words. Neither of them had any clue as to what was really going on.

"Alex, you have imprisoned me for six months to get me away from Rosa because you love her. I understand this. I promise I will stay away from you forever if you let me be free." She kissed his shoes to show that she was willing to give into anything he wanted. She would do anything to be free.

He reached out and grabbed her hair, spitting in her face. "You disgusting woman. Did you bring me here to show me this writing, huh? What have you done with Rosa? You know how much I love her, I will not tolerate anyone who treats her badly."

Emma sobbed and sobbed. "Alex, please! You put me in here yourself to punish me, so that I would stay away from Rosa. You wrote these words. What has happened to you? I remember clearly what happened that night. Don't you remember? Have you lost your mind?"

Alex thought Emma was deluded and that she was the one who had actually lost her mind. His own mind was in turmoil. He reached around the room for something to kill Emma with, feeling desperate to see her blood. He had never felt so angry in all his life. He looked into the kitchen and saw some knives in a block. He ran into the room and grabbed one tightly in his hand, but he stopped when he saw the suicide note above the sink. He read the instructions on it and became even more enraged.

"Suicide! Suicide?" he said, clutching the knife tighter in his hand. He turned back towards Emma, his eyes like a madman. "Shall I kill myself? Huh?" He gave a psychotic smile. "Good! I will kill myself."

Emma was terrified; she didn't know what Alex was capable of, but she feared he could easily commit any crime right now. She was bemused by his reaction to the notes he'd seen, when she was sure he' been the person who'd written these in the first place. She thought this was the end for her. She felt as though her young life was going to tragically end, and no one would ever know what had happened to her.

Emma screamed for her life, but she knew that her pleas would have no effect on this man; he was like an animal.

Sweaty and shaking, Alex dragged Emma to the corner of the room and stared at her. "I will cut you into bits and pieces before I kill myself, do you get that?" He spat in her face again. She screamed but no one could hear.

"Listen to me," he said quietly but menacingly. She nodded. "Whatever I ask, you tell me the truth. Every time you lie to me, I will cut a piece from your body,. Don't lie to me, and I won't hurt you."

He slowly dragged the knife down her face, towards her neck and shoulder, and he kept going towards her left hand, without drawing blood. When he reached her wrist, he pressed the knife against it, causing Emma intense pain. He ignored her begging. A little blood seeped out.

His memory was returning bit by bit. He was remembering that it was his wedding day, and this incensed him even more.

"Do you know which day you have deprived me of? Do you? What do you want from me?" muttered Alex, grinding his teeth.

"I swear to God, Alex, I don't want anything from you. I don't understand what's going on. On my life, I don't know."

"Okay, you are not listening," he said. "I will repeat once more. If you lie to me, I will show you more of your own blood." He rested the knife on her hand.

Emma didn't know what to do. Should she lie and say she did know something? Was there anything that would make him stop? She insisted again that she knew nothing, and he cut her hand a little more. Red liquid jetted out, and Emma screamed.

Then, suddenly in the background, Alex heard the door

open. He ran with the knife, but he couldn't see anyone. All he could see was some carrier bags, filled with vegetables and bread. Alex tentatively inspected the bags to see exactly what was in there.

He looked around, his face and clothes soaked with sweat, and he saw the door with "Number 2" written on it was open, and that the door with "Number 1" written on it was closed.

The food in the hall was between the two doors. With his heart racing, he looked around at the walls and doors to see if there was any kind of handle to get out. He pushed and kicked every surface he could reach.

Then Alex noticed the words on the paper hanging on the door, which revealed that he had been imprisoned and that he needed to quickly take the food. He felt like his brain was melting out of his ears.

Alex grabbed the food to bring it into the cellar and found another note under the bags. His fingers tore it open as he let out frantic burst of breath.

It read, "Alex, welcome to the new place. You have been imprisoned. It is not possible for you to escape. Emma has also been imprisoned. You will both live here from today until the day your draw your last breath. The other option was to kill you, so please appreciate what you have and that we have kept you alive. Good luck to you in everything."

Alex's face was the colour of porcelain. His knees buckled underneath him as he struggled to breathe. He was confused and couldn't take everything in, and thought there had to be a way to find out what was wanted from him.

At that moment, the door closed hard. Alex's breathing

quickened, and he ran towards the bathroom and began frantically washing his face with ice cold water to try to cool down. The airflow into his mouth was erratic.

He still wasn't sure if he could trust Emma, who was now slumped in the corner bleeding and moaning. Alex moved towards her and sat in front of her weak body. He took her hand and elevated it to stop some of the blood. Emma was still terrified and scrambled to try to get away from him, but she didn't have much strength.

Alex softened his face and voice a little. "How long you have been here?"

Her voice struggled to say, "Six months and five or six days."

Alex urgently looked around the room to find a piece of material or something to cover her wound. He found a first aid kit in the kitchen, took it back to her, and unpacked some antiseptic. He started cleaning the wound delicately and proceeded to tightly tie a dressing around it.

He surveyed the room, trying to find evidence of how long she'd been there. "How do you know that? How do you know how long you've been here?"

She tentatively pointed to her wristwatch in the corner of the room. Alex grabbed the watch, but it didn't have the date on it. "How do you know the actual days?" he asked.

"You put me in here on 02-08-1974, and I have recorded the days ever since, on the wall," she said, pointing to her markings. Her voice was barely audible as she struggled to keep her consciousness.

He stumbled to the wall and looked through all the dates. He wondered if his mind was playing tricks on him.

Was he dreaming? Was he dead? Had he gone insane? Why was she saying that he put her there?

He looked at his own watch and compared it to Emma's and saw they were the same. He didn't know what was going on, but he decided to write his own date down too. He hoped to god that he would not be there six hours, let alone the six months Emma had been there.

"Jesus Christ, what is happening?" he shouted at the ceiling.

Back at the wedding, the party was in full swing. Guests were overawed with the efforts of Alex and the family. Antonio and Rosa had the experience of a lifetime and were relieved that all the strain of the last couple of years was now over for them. They could start believing in their new life together. They wanted lots of children who would bring them happiness forever. "I can't wait to have a young Antonio running around!" Rosa said cheekily to her new husband. He giggled dreamily.

Meanwhile, Clara and Jean cleaned themselves up and made their way to the wedding. When they arrived, they found Robert straight away. Clara took him into a corner and whispers in his ear, "Many congratulations, Robert – everything has been worth it for your son and for this moment, hasn't it? I'm so glad we have been able to help you with your mission."

Robert smiled at Clara and Jean with all his love. "I will always be successful in my life when I have you. I thank you from the bottom of my heart. Although I will never forgive you for bringing me that coffin at the last party – I will never forget that," he said, his tongue partly in cheek.

They all danced together for a little while and drank some more champagne, enjoying the light atmosphere after the intense events earlier in the day.

The rest of the day was everything the family could wish for, with wonderful food, music, and frivolity. The speeches were perfect, and Antonio remembered that he needed to be the Alex the whole time.

That night, when he and Rosa were alone together, he could be the real Antonio once more, and it felt good.

At midnight, he took Rosa up to their room, which contained a four-poster bed and silk sheets that was sprinkled with rose petals. It smelled of warm citrus and vanilla, Rosa's favourite scents, and the room was lit with traditional candlesticks.

Antonio had ordered chilled chocolate cocktails for them on arrival, and in the background, a tape of Rosa's favourite songs played.

Their night together was magical. They pushed any thoughts of Alex to the back of their minds and enjoyed each other's bodies for hours.

Alex's mind raced in his prison. He would lie on the floor for hours at a time, feeling numb, and then he'd scream for a while and go quiet again. He kept repeating this, feeling like he was in a mental asylum; it was the same as Emma had felt when she first arrived.

His head searched for explanations. He wondered whether Rosa had been imprisoned somewhere else and hoped they could be reunited. But there were no answers.

Over the next few weeks, Emma and Alex discussed the situation each day, asking one another questions. They were still highly suspicious of each other because there was no other explanation for what had happened, other than that they had done this to each other.

Emma was sure that Alex had kidnapped her and put her in the underground, and Alex thought that given the nature of the notes and the way they were warning him not to think about Rosa, Emma must have been involved in all this. They began to be more and more civil to each other and eventually discussed their lives in the outside world in more depth.

After spending few days together as husband and wife, Antonio returned to Alex's job completely in character. His staff was fully convinced by his impersonation, and he didn't find it too hard. Sometimes he would study the videos again at night to refresh himself on how Alex acted.

Although he passed as Alex, he had a few problems with the workload at the bank. There had been a big build-up of folders while Alex had been away, and so there was a substantial deluge of work for Antonio to catch up on. He struggled to understand the complexity of what he had to do and how to get through it in the correct way.

He asked his supervisors to help him and tried to find excuses not to do the work because it was such a struggle for him. He was also taking work home and getting Clara and Jean to help him through it in the evenings. They were very supportive, but it was taking over his whole life when he just wanted to relax with Rosa in the evenings. He wanted to go to the theatre with her, go for nice dinners. He wanted them to go for walks and appreciate each other.

It was not a good start to his new role. Additionally, he often forgot how angry and miserable Alex could be at work and didn't remember to put the staff in their place or make them fearful of him. He was not the angry person Alex was, and he found it hard to keep reminding himself to be mean.

The workers beneath him assumed that married life had changed him, mellowed him and made him a happier, friendlier person. They were, of course, pleased to see this; it meant they could feel much more comfortable and contented at work. The bank was a happier place to be, even if Antonio still needed time to fully know the job as well as Alex did.

In the underground prison, Emma had felt much better since Alex arrived, even though the situation was horrible at first. They were starting to be nicer to each other, and for her, a lot of the loneliness had been removed by him being there. She had hated being alone, just sitting there with nothing to do and no one to talk to; it was truly the bleakest existence.

She had yearned to be this close to him for so long; her body had ached for Alex, and now he had no choice but to be with her every day. They were stuck with each other.

She often tried to talk to him about the intense love she felt for him, even if she still thought he was the one who did this to her. She was slowly having to forgive him and didn't want to put too much pressure on him to explain himself because she knew this would just annoy him, and the atmosphere would become even more sour and depressing.

For Clara and Jean, life was very good indeed. They were

busy doing their work and missed their families, but they tried to see them when they could, and they received lots of bonuses from Robert when they did extra work.

Robert felt indebted to them for all their efforts in executing his plan so meticulously and professionally. They were worth every penny of their salary, and they were also like family in a way.

One year later and Emma and Alex were getting on better than ever. They had resigned themselves to being stuck underground, although they always hoped that someday they would be rescued. They had to be a source of comfort to each other, encouraging each other to be strong.

The two of them managed to laugh together and found they had similar views on life. They talked about everything from their childhoods to work, to relationships, and everything in between. They took it in turns cooking for each other and tried to make the best life they could for each other.

Emma began to feel as though she would rather be in the underground with Alex than in the outside world without him. It was a strange feeling; she felt now as if she couldn't ever be without him again, and they were so used to each other.

Alex, however, still thought about Rosa every day. He missed her soft hair and smooth skin, her voice and her smile. He couldn't stop thinking about her. Every morning, he would wonder what she was doing.

He marked down each birthday, anniversary, and every other important date in his life – many he would have celebrated with Rosa. Emma did the same and thought about her family and friends. She found it difficult to hear about Rosa, but she understood Alex's feelings as much as she could.

Over time, they began to feel less and less connected to their outside lives; they started to think less frequently about being released and grew to have some acceptance their existence. It seemed that was the only way to stop themselves going completely out of their minds.

Though Alex clearly still loved Rosa, because he couldn't be with her, he became increasingly attached to Emma.

One cold evening, Alex was sitting on the floor, looking at the dates on the wall, reminiscing about his childhood – and wondering whether he would ever have any children of his own. He remembered the games his dad played with him and gently laughed.

Candlelight illuminated the wall and cast a shadow across his peaceful face. The candle was in the corner of the room, next to Emma. She was sat with her legs crossed under her, and her head resting against the wall. She kept looking over to Alex, studying his features.

She finally said, "Alex, you know when you love someone?" She pauses, and he turns around.

"Yes?"

She looked into his hazel green eyes. "You will do anything for them. You do ridiculous things, and you can't help yourself."

Alex knew Emma was talking about her love for him, and he wanted to take her seriously; he sat quietly listening to her.

"I spent so many lonely nights down here before you

came along. I still don't know whether you put me here, but even so, it doesn't change my feelings. I don't think anything you could do would change how I feel about you. I don't know why that is." She shed a few tears and paused for a few seconds, feeling silly. "What is wrong with me, Alex? Why don't you love me like I love you? I would give everything to you, do anything for you." She pulled a tissue from her pocket and dabbed her eyes. She felt deflated because she was not getting what she wanted from Alex.

Alex got up and sat next to her. He wiped her tears with the tissue and kissed each of her eyes. Emma stopped crying for a second and looked up at him. He moved closer to her and put his lips tenderly on hers. They kissed longingly for a few minutes.

It was the moment Emma had been waiting to happen for so many years. Afterwards, neither of them spoke, instead wrapping their arms around each other and sitting in the corner with their eyes closed.

Alex's feelings had changed towards her partly because there was no one else for him to feel affectionate about, no one to be passionate with, and also because he was growing to like her. They had been forced to bond because they were all that each other had in the world right now – and possibly forever.

Two years had passed since the wedding, and Rosa and Antonio's love for one another also grew stronger and stronger every day. Little did they know when they were children that this was the life they would live, but they were grateful to Robert for putting them together, and neither could think of a more perfect existence. They were always very romantic with each other.

For example, on Antonio's birthday, Rosa took him to his favourite opera, *La Fanciulla*, at the Royal Opera House and then to one of the best late-night bars, where they sampled a large selection of international drinks.

The next morning, at 11.30 AM, Rosa and Antonio were still sleeping deeply. They had got in at 3.00 a little tipsy.

The sun was streaming through the thin, purple velvet curtains, which had been left slightly open in the middle after the two of them had fallen into bed.

Rosa moved, and a beam of sunlight hit her eyes, causing her to stir. She groaned and turned over to see Antonio, who was still fast asleep.

She ran her hand seductively through Antonio's hair, and the jet of sun reflected off her engagement ring.

Rosa looked at Antonio amorously and smiled. She kissed him on the forehead, partly enjoying him sleeping and partly wanting him to wake up so she could have fun with him.

She began rubbing his chest, trying to wake him up, but he doesn't move. Rosa put the bed sheet over her head, got on top of her lover, and began touching his stomach softly with her lips, working her way up to his lips. She kissed his mouth for several seconds, and at this point Antonio opened his eyes, and both of them laughed. He swung Rosa onto her back and jumped on top of her to tickle her. They both laughed hysterically.

"Stop it!" said Rosa, laughing flirtatiously.

He released her after a few moments, and they both collapsed on their backs, still giggling.

"We need to get up, darling. Let me make you your favourite brunch," said Rosa, putting on her silk dressing gown and tying her hair back loosely.

Antonio pulled himself out of bed and went to the bathroom for a quick, cold shower to wake himself up. He put on some clean trousers and a shirt on and headed into the kitchen.

Their kitchen was modern, with pristine white cabinets and plenty of space, including a large workstation area and a heavy oak breakfast table in the middle.

The counter surface was filled with ripe, multicoloured fresh fruit, walnut and tomato breads, and meat and cheese, bought by Rosa the day before.

Marvin Gaye played on the stereo, and Rosa stood at the cooker preparing some smoked salmon, quail eggs, and a cress salad. The smell of the walnut bread in the oven filled the house, making Antonio very hungry.

He kissed Rosa's neck and then prepared the table with plates, cutlery, fresh red berry juice, squeezed lemon for the salmon, and creamy butter from Italy.

He walked back to Rosa, kissed her on the back of the head, and put his arms around her waist, holding her tightly.

She smiled, switched off the cooker, and pushed Antonio out of the way with her bum before carrying the food over to the breakfast table. She put it inside the hot plate while they ate some fruit and warm bread.

"Wow, this looks so good, thank you, my love. Cheers to our future," Antonio said as they clinked their orange juice glasses.

"Isn't this perfect?" said Rosa wistfully. They both smiled.

They loved being together, particularly on weekends when Antonio had more time. They also visited Robert in Italy whenever possible and would enjoy wonderful times with him at the holidays. They would all go walking in the mountains for days, living life to the fullest, thinking about their dreams, and talking about the past.

During their second Christmas as a married couple, Robert took the two of them in the Dolomite Mountains, in northeast Italy, via train. Each peak was laden with heavy white snow, and skiers whizzed around with looks of sheer exhilaration on their faces.

The family stayed in a grand log cabin in the mountains overlooking many pretty villages and towns. It had a lively, crimson fire and a real Christmas tree which released an intoxicating pine fragrance all day.

On Christmas day they sat in the local tavern, which was decorated with gold and silver trimmings, and waited for the Christmas lunch. They all wore thick jumpers and sipped on hot mulled wine to fend off the bleak temperatures. Other families sat around the communal fire with their children, singing festive songs and laughing together and trying to keep insulated.

After dinner, a little girl of about six years old came to sit by Rosa and cuddled into her, playing with Rosa's long, dark ringlets. Rosa felt her heart melt. Antonio and Robert smiled at them both and then at each other.

"Rosa," said Robert, looking a little serious. "When are you going to give me some grandchildren? You and Antonio would make fantastic parents. I long for some little ones running around before I'm too old."

Rosa laughed gently. "Well, we would love some little ones too, Father. Wouldn't we, Antonio?" He nodded. "I guess it's just finding the right time," she said. "But we would love to have lots, and you will be a fantastic grandfather!" The corners of her mouth crinkled warmly.

Robert's eyes twinkled. "Marvellous," he said loudly.

"I don't think you'll have to wait too long, don't worry," said Antonio.

The little girl went back to her parents, and they carried on eating their cheese and wine and chatted for several hours into the evening, while a band played jazz in the background.

Robert longed for them to have some grandchildren for

him, and they promised him they would provide some as soon as possible. They were keen to have their own family and thought about this often. They discussed names and what dreams and aspirations they would have for their children.

Two days before Christmas Eve, the couple spent the morning doing a short hike in the mountains before making their way back to the airport to come home. Robert was a little forlorn as he said good-bye. "Please come and see me soon, you two, okay?" he asked.

"Of course we will, Father, we miss you," they replied

Robert made his way back to his home later that day and went to bed feeling a little lonely. Sometimes he thought he might like to have a woman in his life, but he knew that no one could ever replace Antonio's mother.

The next day, Antonio was at work at the bank when he received a phone call from Italy. "Can I call back? I'm just finishing something," said Antonio to the member of staff who'd taken the call.

"Sir, I think you need to take this call," he said, looking very serious.

"Okay, thank you," he said, taking the phone.

"Antonio, please sit down," said a voice at the other end, which he recognised as Robert's chief of staff.

"What is it? Is everything okay? Where's my father?" Antonio said, panicking.

"Antonio, I am so truly sorry to have to tell you this. I'm afraid Robert has had a heart attack. He passed away one hour ago."

Antonio dropped the phone and stared at the ceiling,

slumped in his chair. He was silent. "Sir, can I do anything for you?" said the member of staff who'd taken the call.

Antonio struggled to speak. "Can … you … get … me … Rosa," he poured out in a monotone voice, his hands gripping the desk to stop him from falling.

"Of course, sir, I know you were very close to your father-in-law." Antonio's eyes filled with hot tears as he realised that everyone thought that Robert was not his father. They would probably wonder why he was so desperately sad, but he had no control over his emotions. There was no way he would be able to hide the extent of his sadness.

Antonio got a taxi home, and he and Rosa sat down and hugged each other, crying for the next few hours. "How could this happen so suddenly? He seemed so well when we saw him," said Rosa.

She did not expect an answer because there wasn't one. Robert had simply been taking a morning stroll when he'd collapsed. There was nothing anyone could have done, the staff told them. Antonio's soul ached. "He will never see his grandchildren," cried Antonio into Rosa's hair.

They were both painfully exhausted and cried for hours before falling asleep in each other's arms on the sofa.

The next morning, they packed a few essentials and took a flight back to Italy with Jean, for Robert's burial. Clara stayed to look after the store. They hadn't expected to be returning so soon, and not for such a heartbreaking occasion.

The three of them hardly spoke on the journey. Jean tried to offer some words of comfort, but he didn't really know what to say. They mostly stayed silent. Rosa was wearing dark glasses to hide her swollen eyes, and she was unable to speak to staff on the plane, keeping her head low.

When they arrived, they found the whole neighbourhood dressed in black for mourning. Locals wanted to show their respect for a much-loved man. "It is all too sudden, so final," said Antonio to Jean and Rosa as they arrived in the town. "I feel so empty."

Rosa wrapped herself around him, her tears soaking his shirt. Jean put an arm around him. "I'm so sorry, it is the most terrible loss," said the assistant. "There can be no one that will ever replace your father. He was such a remarkable man; this town will never be the same."

Hundreds of people turned up to the funeral and the wake, organised by Robert's staff. Everyone tried to talk to Antonio and Rosa, but the two of them found it difficult to respond.

They just stood in dark glasses, saying their prayers for most of the day. Before the body was buried, Antonio was called by the minister to give a speech for his father. He had planned something, but he didn't know if he had the strength to deliver it.

He solemnly walked to Robert's graveside and cleared his throat. He took his glasses off and looked at the crowds.

"Thank you all ... for coming," he said in broken speech. "It would have meant so much to my father to see the support he has. My father was a gentleman and did much for other people, as you know. It was his wish that charities were supported with his money and people made well.

"I ask you to today appreciate all he has done and all that

he never got to do, and to always have love in your hearts, as he did. I will never forget this man, who did so much for me and Rosa. I hope God will look after him. Thank you."

Antonio tried his best to finish the speech for his father; he wanted to make him proud, for him to smile down from heaven. He struggled, but he received a round of applause and Rosa was very grateful to him. The funeral staff were the same ones who thought they had buried Antonio several years earlier.

Robert was buried next to the person who was supposed to be Antonio, in a local cemetery. It was beautiful, with many flowers and trees. "One day, we will bring our children here," said Rosa to Antonio, stroking his hand.

He hugged her tightly. "I'm so glad I have you, Rosa. I don't know what I would do without you, I can't ever imagine it. Please never leave me."

"Don't ever speak of this," said Rosa. "There is no need to ever think that. Promise me you will never say that again." She stared at him.

"I swear, Rosa. I just love you so much." He put his head in his hands, and they both stood in the graveyard and cried for awhile.

The two of them stayed in Italy for the next night, emotionally looking through their father's things, before returning back to London the next day.

On the journey, they talked in-depth about going back to Italy permanently to look after Robert's wealth and property as stated in the plan. Of course, the original plan stated that Antonio would have the wealth, not Alex, but as Rosa's husband he was entitled to it.

He registered for his inheritance in Alex's name as soon as he got back to London, and they both began making arrangements for their new life in Italy.

Every task reminded them painfully of Robert. They often broke down and cried in each other's arms, realising that they would never see him again. Rosa carried a photo of herself and Robert in her purse and would look at it at night, stroking Robert's face gently.

In the underground, Emma and Alex's love for each other was further deepened, and their attachment was now very powerful.

They were as romantic as they could be, despite being locked up in a cellar. They gave each other massages and ran each other candlelit baths.

One evening, Alex was in the bathroom washing shampoo out of his hair when Emma entered the bathroom sneakily and closed the bathroom door without making any noise.

She walked over to the bath, where Alex was lying in the hot water with his eyes closed. He sensed something and opened his eyes to see Emma in front of him. She looked into his eyes and suggestively dropped her towel before stepping into the water. She leaned over him, and they kissed as the hot steam off the bath erotically wrapped around their bodies. They touched each other's skin all over, and both felt sensually alive. Alex had never known he could feel like this about Emma. From then on, they enjoyed each other's bodies regularly, becoming closer and closer.

A couple of months later, Emma woke up feeling ill with pains in her stomach. She went to the sink and vomited three times. This happened several times over the next few weeks, and Emma realised that her period had also stopped.

She called Alex to the bathroom one morning. "God, Alex, I think I'm having a baby. Oh my God," she said, partly stunned but party happy.

"What? What? Are you sure?" said Alex. His head felt cloudy.

"I'm not sure, but it seems really likely," she replied.

"Well, are you going to be okay? This could be something exciting for us, but how will we have a baby here, in this hole?" Alex asked.

"I don't know," said Emma, gently falling into a heap on the floor and looking rough. "Perhaps they will feel sorry for us and let us out of here."

Alex hugged her and tried to reassure her things would be okay, even though he was not at all sure that things would actually be ok for them. He was quite scared of them having a baby in the underground, but he was also excited about being a father.

They started thinking about names for their child. Although they didn't know whether it would be a boy or a girl, Alex insisted that if it was a girl they should call her Rosa, because she had been a loyal name in his life and he felt it was his only way to keep Rosa's memory alive and somewhere in the bottom of his heart. Emma naturally did not like the idea of this, but she loved Alex so much that she went along with it.

They also started to make some clothes for the baby, from Alex's old clothes. Emma had also been wearing Alex's clothes, because their captors hadn't thought about her clothing needs.

The next few months were difficult. Emma was in pain a lot, receiving no fresh air and no medical treatment. She was not very healthy. They became increasingly scared about having the child, but on the other hand it was the only thing they had to look forward to

Every time they received food, they left a note to say that they needed to go to the hospital, but the notes were just left where they were; it seemed as though they weren't even being read.

Nine months passed, as marked on the chart, and they were still trapped, terrified of how they would deliver this baby on their own. It was a week after the nine months had passed when Emma awoke sharply in the middle of the night, screaming in pain. She was sweating and breathing heavily.

Alex was panicking. He wiped Emma's head with a cold wet towel and got her some water. He took some deep breaths himself and tried to offer Emma some comforting words. He wondered how long it would be before he saw the baby; he'd heard about labour periods lasting more than a day.

"Alex, I need help," screamed Emma in agony. "I need pain killers, I need a hospital, I need a nurse."

Alex was so frustrated. He was angrily kicking and punching the walls because he couldn't do anything to help Emma or his child. He was incensed that someone could leave them here to have a baby with no support or medical attention.

Alex could only do what he had seen in the movies, and that was to say "push" to Emma. But she was making so much noise, she couldn't even hear him.

Just after 3.00 AM, their baby girl was born and looked

healthy. Alex was so happy that Emma and the baby were okay. "It is a beautiful girl with bright eyes. She is amazing," he said happily. Emma was exhausted but smiled with tears in her eyes. She held the baby close to her while it gently cried.

Emma let Alex call her Rosa, even though it was not her choice and they both felt a sense of contentment about having her; it gave them a purpose in life. There could be no more thoughts of killing themselves to escape, because they had someone else to think about and take care of.

This also meant they had to provide good food for their young one, and therefore they had to reduce their own consumption. The food they received was a good amount, and Alex and Emma were a little hungry at first, but they adjusted to less at meal times.

It was clear that their captors would provide no more food, and so Alex and Emma knew that there was no way they could have another child because they would all be starving. They had to be very careful.

They recorded Rosa's weeks and months on the wall and enjoyed seeing her grow. It made them sad that she had no real toys, but they did their best to entertain her, telling her stories and having fun with whatever was around the underground.

But as the baby's first birthday approached, Alex and Emma felt so terribly sad that they had nothing to give her to celebrate. They were forced to realise that it would get worse as she got older, with no fresh air around, nowhere to run and play, and no other children.

Alex did his best to create a new dress for her, to prepare some special food, and to light some candles. It was their way of celebrating, and Rosa seemed happy and giggly, almost like a normal little girl.

In their own house, Rosa and Antonio had spent a lot of time wrapping up their work and business in Britain, in order to return to Italy. His staff would miss the new "Alex" he'd become since the wedding, and Rosa and Antonio would both miss London. But they were looking forward to their new life back in Italy, where they belonged.

However, there was one big problem. Clara and Jean would have to go with them because they were the people who knew all about Robert's dealings and businesses in depth. Antonio did know about some of the work, but not in the way the other two did, and he would need them to be there with him all the time.

But, of course, this would mean that no one would be available to see to Alex and Emma's needs. There was no one they could trust outside the group to help them with this.

Antonio, Clara, and Jean talked for weeks about what to do, going through any options they thought might be possible. But nothing seemed possible. They only option that seemed as though it would work was something that wouldn't have been possible before Robert's death – to kill Alex and Emma.

Rosa of course would never approve, and so they could not tell her of this. Clara and Jean assured Antonio that this was the only option and that he should not waste any more time in arranging what they had decided.

The next day, the three of them disguised themselves in dark but inconspicuous costumes, with hats and masks.

They were able to see out of the masks, but no one was able to see in or recognise them. They each carried a gun in their trousers.

The quickly ran from their car into the store after checking nobody was looking and then they flung the door of the underground prison open. Clara ran in, hyper alert and ready to shoot, but she was startled to see the little girl playing behind the door. She gasped and dropped her guard as the baby began crawling towards them. Little Rosa had never seen any other people before and was intrigued by these new figures that had appeared. She crawled even closer, mesmerised and trying to talk.

The three of them stood still, looking at each other helplessly, not knowing what to do. Antonio deeply regretted what he'd come to do after seeing the child, but he didn't know what else he should do.

Emma and Alex heard the door and leapt to the child, only to find three dark figures with guns. They were beyond terrified, and both dropped to the ground to grab Rosa.

Jean screamed, "Don`t move forward, or I will kill you." Antonio instantly aimed his handgun towards Emma and Alex as a reflex reaction. They looked petrified, their bodies quivering while they tried to stay still.

Then Emma reached out and yelled, "Please don't touch my daughter."

Antonio faced Emma, himself panicking. "Don't move!"

Emma kneeled, crying with both of her hands on her chest, begging them.

Alex screamed, "Please don't shoot, please don't hurt my daughter."

Rosa was startled and began wailing like a distraught animal. Clara picked her up and held her, trying to soothe her amongst the commotion.

All Antonio could think about was that he wanted to get out of the place. He didn't want to be a part of this anymore. He wanted it to all be over. But he didn't know what choice was left. "Move and I will kill you," he shouted to Alex. "I came here to kill you, I'm so sorry, I have to kill you."

Emma pleaded with Clara to get the baby back. She was on her hands and knees, feeling as though her heart was splitting.

"Who are you? What do you want from us?" Alex said ferociously.

"Shut up," said Jean angrily, aiming the gun at his face.

Antonio then spoke. "I am Alex, and I am sure that you don't want your daughter to die; that is why we are going to take her with us. We promise that we are going to bring her up for you and look after her."

Emma became even more agitated, like a crazed patient in a metal hospital. She was hysterical. "No! For God's sake, no! What do you want from us? Please leave us alone!"

Jean spoke loudly, "If you move any nearer, I will kill you." He put the gun near the child's head.

The little girl screamed, crying, "Mama, Mama" over and over again.

"Please, my daughter, please," Emma whispered. She could hardly see from tears, and her neck was wet with salt water.

"It is no use begging," said Jean. "We will have to kill you." He then indicated that Clara take the child away.

Alex was in utter despair. "Please let me hold my baby once more, so she can have a lasting memory of me as her father. Please, please. Oh God."

Emma dared not move in case they shot. She was crying her heart out and pulling her hair tightly.

Antonio really wished he hadn't gone to the underground. He was devastated about the barbaric crimes he was there to commit for the sake of his own future, and he knew his father would not approve of him murdering people. And he himself had always been seen as a loyal and generous person. What would people think if they knew he was about to kill a mother and father after the torture he had put them through? What would people say about him making a child an orphan?

He tried his hardest to be tough, to be in control of the situation and do what he'd set out to do. But holding back on mercy, he said to Alex, "No, I'm going to have to kill you, I'm sorry."

Alex asked again, "Please! If you have to kill me, just let me smell my child and say good-bye to her." He breathed deeply, sobbing. "Surely even my wildest enemy wouldn't deprive me of that?"

Emma rocked herself back and forth, repeating over and over, "God help us." The baby continued to cry.

Antonio looked at Emma and indicated to the baby. "Come and take it," he said.

Emma and Antonio ran to Rosa and kissed and hugged her all over. They didn't know if they would ever see her again, and their minds were dark with thoughts of what these people might do to her after they were gone.

Rosa was hysterical, her cries filling the room. Antonio was finding it all unbearable.

Jean shouted with venom, "If you don't give her back, I will kill her with you, got it?"

They both struggled to let go of her, but Alex was terrified they would maim Rosa, and so he took her from Emma and gave her back to Clara.

Emma continued to wail, her eyes bulging out of her head with the crying. Alex tried to go back to the baby, but Antonio told him to leave her and pointed to Clara to take her again.

Alex looked at the child and kissed her forehead. He hugged her tightly. "I will miss you, Rosa. I hope that you will keep Rosa's name and hold your head high. I don't know if you will remember this, but you were named after a beautiful woman whom I loved deeply. You are Princess Rosa," he wept, controlling his tears, so he could talk to Rosa properly.

"If you see Rosa, the woman I named you after, tell her our pledge and about what has happened to us. For now, good-bye, my daughter." He kissed her on both hands and restrained himself from crying more.

Antonio was overwhelmed when he heard that the baby had been called Rosa. It suddenly dawned on him that his Rosa was an orphan who had no memory of her real mother and father. He thought about how many times she'd talked to him about how lost she felt because she didn't know her family. She longed just to see a photo of them. He didn't want to make another orphaned Rosa, and he knew that his

Rosa would be upset beyond belief if he went through with his intended actions.

"Stop," said Antonio. "Give them back the child. Don't kill them."

Jean and Clara looked at each other and then looked at Antonio. They put the girl back on the ground and left the room.

Emma and Alex leapt to her and held her, laughing and crying at the same time. Their little girl had just saved their lives. Even if they were both suffering and depressed, this was becoming one of the best and most sacred days of their life. They fell to their knees and thanked God for freeing them from death.

They had given up hope of ever trying to have a normal life – to have more children, to breathe clean air, to be able send Rosa to school. They wondered if they would run out of space to record their days at some point in the future.

Antonio's mind felt beaten by his actions, and he knew his father would turn in his grave if he'd known. He wondered how he could have even contemplated trying to kill an innocent man and woman and making their child an orphan, all in his own interest.

Alex had called Antonio barbaric, and he knew Alex was right. He was from one of the most loved and respected families in Italy. How could he ever have thought of doing such things? He tensed his arms and fingers and hit his head against the cellar wall repeatedly, as though he was having a mental breakdown. He squeezed his hands tightly so they hurt. He wanted to punish himself.

He turned to Clara and Jean, who were standing still quietly waiting for his orders, unsure of what he was going to do next. He turned to them, his face dripping with hot sweat, his cheeks as red as fresh blood. With hate in his eyes, he said defiantly, "Why have you made this happen? Never, ever make me a plan like this for me again. Do you understand? Look at what you have done." He was out of breath. They both continued to stay still and just nodded, worried about his hysteria.

"Listen to me. My father's advice can't be ignored. You understand?"

He had never spoken to them with such authority before, but he had never felt this strongly about the plan.

"Your father worked throughout your life, so that you could inherit everything," said Jean timidly.

Antonio screamed, making them all jump. "No! There is no killing in my father's plan!"

Clara interrupted, quietly, "We are here to help you."

He raged back, throwing his hands in the air. "With the killing and torture of innocent people, huh? To make another child with the name of Rosa orphaned?"

"We don't have any other solutions, Antonio. We can't set them free. Sooner or later they will have to vanish," Jean tried to reason.

Antonio shook his head disapprovingly and bit his lip. "No, you will stay in London to watch them and to manage the commercial business at the same time, until we find another solution.?"

They all agreed that this is what would happen, and

then they left the family in the cellar to try to return back to a normal life.

When Antonio arrived home, he had to lie to Rosa and say he'd had an accident to cover up for the way he looked and the way he was acting. He was relieved to see her and held her tightly after he'd bathed, wishing memories of the day would wash away. That night he had horrific dreams of death and torture and kept waking up. Rosa had to keep calming him down.

"My love, what has happened to you?" she said, stroking his head. "I've never seen you like this before. Has something bad happened? What is in your head?"

"I don't know," he said breathlessly. "I think I was just dreaming about Father. It's upset me." He hugged her tightly, feeling guilty. He was partly telling the truth because he knew his father would disapprove of what he'd almost done."

The next day Rosa and Antonio went into central London for a romantic day together, sorting out what they needed to go back to Italy. It was a rainy, cloudy day, but they hardly noticed, laughing and joking together, chatting about life and what they would miss about London. Antonio was glad to have the previous day's events behind him. He concentrated on enjoying their time together.

They were happier than ever to be together and bought each other little presents throughout the day. They were like a couple who had just met and were always considerate of each other.

After a special dinner together at a beautiful hotel overlooking Hyde Park, they decided to walk to the taxi rank to relax. They ambled through the quiet, winding streets, stopping to listen to a busker playing love songs before carrying on towards the taxis.

They came to a zebra crossing to go over the busy main road and stood for a moment. As they were waiting for the cars to stop, Antonio caught an old blind man trying to cross the road in the wrong place further down the road. The man seemed confused.

"Oh, that poor man. Can you wait for me while I help him cross?" said Antonio to Rosa.

"Of course, you are such a good man, always helping people." She let him go and continued to cross the road with their carrier bags.

The man was very grateful as Antonio took his arm and began to lead him to the crossing safely

But as Rosa got halfway over the crossing, a speeding car screeched around the roundabout and slammed straight into her.

There was a mass of commotion as the car came to a halt, creating a trail of destruction. As he dropped the blind man's hand and ran to Rosa, without realising it, Antonio was calculating that it looked like the car had been going at least fifty or sixty miles an hour. He was absolutely distraught. He howled out, "Call an ambulance!"

Rosa's body was jolted into the air and landed on the ground with a thud; blood poured out of her mouth. Antonio put his left hand under her head and lifted her up, holding her hands with his right. He saw her eyes look at him for a few seconds and then close. She had disappeared, passed away before his eyes.

"Please, Rosa, please stay with me," he said, kissing her

head and face, dripping tears all over her bloodless skin. But she was gone, and he fell to her side and hugged her body tightly, howling his eyes out.

People gathered around them, and police sirens and ambulances could be heard in the distance. When the ambulance arrived and picked up Rosa's body, Antonio got up and kicked and punched the car and hit his head against the window. He kept screaming. He wanted to kill the driver of the vehicle that hit his love.

Antonio dragged the driver out of the car and started beating him within an inch of his life. "I'll kill you, you bastard. What have you done? You have ruined my life. I will strangle you, I swear!"

The crowds dragged him off, and he fought to get away from them and run to the ambulance to be with Rosa. His clothes torn and bloodied, he climbed in and clung to her body, like a mother clinging to her baby.

It was the worst disaster imaginable. Antonio couldn't believe all this time spent on this plan and his life crashed down around him. He had nothing left; his heart was in a million pieces. He sobbed as he held on to her head. "My poor Rosa, my poor, dear Rosa, I shouldn't have left you. I will never forgive myself. I love you, Rosa."

She was taken to the hospital, but her body was pronounced dead on arrival. Antonio sat there for hours in the hospital and cried himself to sleep in a chair. Rosa's body was taken for forensic tests, and he went home and shut himself away from the world.

For a few weeks, Antonio locked himself in his room and would not speak to anyone or answer the phone. He just slept and cried all day, feeling he had nothing left to live for. He could not see the point in life anymore. He only ate small bits of bread and water all day and became very thin and pale quickly, with deep, black circles under his sunken eyes.

His two assistants came to see him every day to encourage him to eat and wash, but he didn't let them in. The bank staff tried to bring flowers and food and offer support, but he wasn't interested. He was empty with Rosa's memory all around him. He was wounded inside and didn't know if he would recover. He slept very little, with constant nightmares about the accident when he closed his eyes.

At the bank, the staff tried to cover him and do his work where possible, but they were finding it difficult to cope without him, and they missed him as a person too. They sent him letters offering support, be he didn't read them.

Antonio was getting weaker and more desperate by day; his hair and beard grew long and scruffy, and he had stopped washing. He looked as though he had been sleeping roughly, if at all.

In his mind, he kept going over and over what had happened the day Rosa died and also his actions with Alex and Emma. He felt as if God might be punishing him brutally for his behaviour. He thought he deserved what had happened. Alex had done nothing wrong.

He started to feel as if there really was karma. If he did something bad, something bad would happen back to him. He stood in the mirror and cried and crumbled in front of his own eyes. He was not worthy of calling himself a man anymore.

He looked awful. When he had been doing good things

with his life, he'd always looked bright and happy in front of the mirror. "I will never look happy again," he said to himself.

In the outside world, Clara and John didn't know whether to call a doctor for Antonio, but they were concerned about his health and mental state. One morning, after hours of trying to talk to him from outside his door, they convinced him to let them in. They panicked when they saw his eyes so bloodshot, and his very long beard. They barely recognised him; he looked like a shadow of himself.

Clara was so sad to see him like this. Jean hugged him tightly and said, "Antonio, my God, what has happened?" He put his hand on his shoulder: "It is so heartbreaking for you. I know Rosa didn't deserve this. I wish I could bring her back for you."

"I know, I know," said Antonio. He was so lost, he sounded like a child. "I just don't want to live without her."

"Antonio, don't speak like this. Your father worked so hard for you; you must continue to look after his wealth and estate, and you need to be fit to do this. We will get you some medical help, we need to make you better. We can do it," assured Jean.

Jean and Clara spent hours to find someone to come the next day to clean the house and make the atmosphere a bit more bearable for Antonio, reorganising the house and making him as comfortable as possible. The bought him fresh food and clothes and hoped he would clean himself up a bit.

"Antonio," Jean said tentatively, "we are going to need

some help with sorting out Rosa's burial. We need to talk about what you want; this can't go on much longer. There is no point in you being isolated here because it won't bring your beloved back, and we need to arrange a proper funeral for her."

After much persuasion, Antonio reluctantly agreed to return back to work and help arrange Rosa's funeral. He never wanted to have to think about arranging his wife's funeral at such a young age. He also asked them to arrange a meeting for the next morning with the bank staff, to thank them for their support.

Clara and Jean were very happy with this news, and Clara went straight to the bank to inform the staff that Alex would return back to work the next morning and that there would be a short meeting before he resumed work the following week. It was Saturday the next day, but the staff was okay with coming in because they were concerned and felt sorry for Alex.

They were all very sad about Rosa, because it was clear to them that Rosa had completely changed him into a gentleman who was quiet and reserved and helpful to them whenever he could be.

The staff prepared to brief Antonio, whom they thought was Alex, and update him on what had been happening over the last month.

The next morning, Antonio woke up very early to go to the bank.

The velvet curtain was almost fully drawn, and the rain drizzled down on the window. The sky was a dirty shade of grey. It would be a glum day, even for someone who was happy. The little bit of light coming from the window hit a picture on the dresser near the window, which had a crack through it.

Antonio's was lying on the bed, his face is drawn. He turned around and looked at the empty pillow next to him, staring through it. He strained to see out of his swollen eyes. His gaze wandered towards the dresser next to the window, where the cracked picture of him and Rosa on their wedding day sat.

He dragged his aching body from the bed, unable to look at the picture anymore. He stumbled into the kitchen and took a soiled plate and glass from a grim sink full of unwashed items.

The workstation was virtually empty except for some old bread and rotten peaches. He opened the fridge, and the smell almost knocked him out. There was a chocolate tart at the front – with green fur starting to cover it. He shut the door and headed into the living room. There was little light coming through, and the coldness hung in the air. The house was so empty without his wife.

He took a pen and some paper out of the draw and wrote the following letter to his two assistants.

> Dear Clara and Jean
> I am thankful to you – you were my father's truly faithful friends and were also very dear to Rosa and me. You have always been greatly admired in all your efforts to achieve my father's plans, and to fulfil our dreams. But I urge you to now return back to your relatives and have a happy life with your families. Try to bring your children up with good manners, but without any conditions and grand plans.

I wish you a prosperous life; may good luck be
with you, and please free my lookalike.

With my respect,

Antonio Robert

He then pulled some old clothes on and took his
handgun and left the house. He looked dishevelled to say
the least. It was 6.00 AM. Antonio got a taxi to the bank
because he couldn't face the walk – he didn't really want any
more thinking time. The taxi driver looked him up and down
cautiously before he let him in the car. They didn't speak
throughout the journey.

Antonio let himself into the bank with his keys and
found rows and rows of chairs lined up in the hall outside
his office. A podium and stage area had been made at the
front for him to stand on for his speech. He felt nervous as he
walked around the chairs, thinking deeply about what would
happen in that room. He rehearsed what he would say over
and over in his head.

He went into his office and locked the door behind him.
It was similar to how he had left it, but there was a bunch of
colourful flowers in water on his table. They reminded him of
the flowers at his and Rosa's wedding, and he found himself
fighting back the tears.

He calmly picked up the flowers and saw a small, white
paper note under them. He opened it gently, and saw that
inside was written, "Welcome back, sir. We are pleased to see
you." The names of the staff were written at the bottom.

Antonio sat in his chair and contemplated his life over
the last few years – the secrets he'd kept, the plans he'd
carried, and the innocent people who'd become part of those

plans were etched into his mind. He could not free himself from them. Rosa's memory filled all his thoughts, and images of Emma and Alex kept flashing into his mind. He was guilt-ridden and was tired of feeling this way.

He opened the draws on his desk and took out a pen and paper and started writing. He thought carefully about each word, breathing deeply before every sentence. The manager folded the paper and put it inside a book, which he then placed in the draw.

Soon after Antonio heard chattering and realised the staff were gradually starting to arrive. He was so on edge that he kept walking up and down his office, talking to himself.

Staff sat down one by one, and at 9.30 AM the hall was full. Everyone was chatting amongst themselves, unaware that Alex was in the next room.

"I hear Alex has gone mad since losing his wife," said one. "Is that true?" came a reply. "And his father-in-law died recently too," commented one woman. They all looked concerned as they talked about their boss.

Meanwhile, Clara and Jean knocked on Antonio's door to see if they could help him in anyway and give him a lift to the bank.

They knocked several times, but there was no response. They wondered if he had changed his mind or was still asleep, and so they waited a little longer, pacing up and down the cold concrete steps outside.

At the bank, the staff were becoming agitated and bored of sitting around. At ten o'clock, the deputy manager informed them that they were still waiting for Alex and asked them to be patient a little while longer. The staff fidgeted and chatted about all the things they were planning to do that day and how they would now be late, but they continued to wait.

A few minutes later, the manager's door suddenly opened. The room fell silent and everyone turned to the door. Their faces dropped when they saw what state Antonio was in. He looked bedraggled and ghost-like.

"My God, what has happened to Alex? Has he gone mad?" said one man loudly, echoing everyone else's thoughts.

Antonio was agitated and worried. He slowly raised his right hand slightly as a sort of greeting and walked quietly on to the stage, his face mournful and his head hanging.

Everyone sat still, not knowing what to say. They could only stare directly at the man who used to be their boss but now looked half dead.

He looked around the room, his eyes full of warm tears, his body numb. He inhaled as much oxygen as he could and spoke. "I want to thank you for your presence. I know you were very concerned for me when Rosa said farewell to this world. As you can see, without her, I am not the man I used to be. And to you, I literally am not the man I used to be."

He paused and looked around the room at different people again. "I know that you are all concerned about Alex. Alex is very good man; he is loyal and innocent, and he didn't deserve what has happened to him."

They were bemused as to why he was referring to himself in the third person, but they kept listening, fixated on Antonio, wondering what on earth he would say next.

"Please listen to me and listen well. I have lost the love of my life." He paused and took his pen and paper and started writing a note. A few minutes later, he said, "If I die, I have written here in this note the address of where you can find Alex. You can bring him back here to carry on working as the manager."

As much as they felt sorry for Alex, the staff couldn't help laughing at his ridiculousness. They were joking and whispering to each other. "I never thought I'd see him like this. He needs a psychiatrist," said one of them.

But when he uttered his next sentence, the room fell deadly silent. Trying to hold himself still, he murmured, "You will also find Emma in the same place as Alex. She is not dead; they are together."

A ripple of gasps and screeches could be heard around the room, and expressions of bewilderment appeared on each face.

"What? Emma has been dead nearly four years!" one woman shouted. The room became louder as everyone started questioning Alex's sanity to each other.

He spoke a little louder. "I understand you think I am mad, but I am not; I am telling you the truth. Believe me, I would not make this up. I wish myself it wasn't real. You might remember Alex, he was different than me – he was impatient and he had a scar on his left hand. Do you remember? He was your real manager."

Antonio took out the hand gun under his jacket, and the staff instinctively ducked. It was the first time that many of them had seen a handgun in real life, and now they knew that Alex was really mad. They had no idea what he was capable of and edged further and further away from him.

Antonio shouted angrily, "I am not Alex, I am not Alex!

I am Antonio, the son of the Italian merchant Robert. I am not a manager, I am a merchant."

The room descended into absolute mayhem, with everyone screaming. But they dared not move from their seats in case he shot at them.

Antonio rolled his left sleeve up and shook his arm at them. "Look! Where is Alex's scar? Eh? Can you see it?"

They couldn't see a scar; there was nothing on his hand, and the atmosphere became increasingly tense. "I just want to get out," cried one woman.

Antonio was shaking. He felt so alone at the moment in time. "This was my father's plan. I am asking for your forgiveness now. Alex is your real manager, not Antonio. Please God, forgive my sins."

He closed his eyes and put his handgun on his head defiantly and shot himself with one bullet. His blood and insides spread across the stage and some of the staff, and he fell to the floor with a loud clunk.

There were loud outbursts of hysteria, and people ran in all directions, some out of the room and some to Antonio's body to see if they could save him. But he was gone. There was no pulse, no heart beat, no breathing – nothing.

He was now reunited with Rosa and Robert, away from the world that had caused him so much trauma and pain. "We are so sorry for your pain, sir," said the deputy manager looking over his body.

At the house, Clara and Jean had waited a very long time for Antonio. They sat in their car running through all the possibilities of what might have happened. "We're going to have to break in," said Jean after they had been silent for a few minutes, watching the door of the house.

"Yes" replied Clara. She wondered about what they might find in the house.

Together, they got out of the car and stood outside the door. They stood poised, ready to kick the door in. On the count of three they each launched a leg at the door, which flew off its hinges, and stepped into the dark and dingy house.

"Hello? Hello? Antonio, are you here? Antonio, where are you?" said Clara hopefully.

They searched in each room and in every closet. Antonio was nowhere. They were frantic. "Where the hell is he?" shouted Jean.

"God knows," said Clara. "I'm really worried. Maybe he left early."

Then Clara saw Antonio's note on the table and read it aloud, slowly and precisely.

"We need to get to the bank immediately!" said Jean. They rushed back out of the house and jumped in the car, speeding off to the bank. They cut through traffic and drove up some one-way streets to get to there. Car horns beeped at them and pedestrians shouted, but they kept their speed up, anxious to reach Antonio.

Emma and Alex had no idea of the dramatic events that were unfolding in the outside world, no idea that people now knew they were alive and in a secret location. They were just playing quietly with their little girl as they did every day. They rarely thought about being let free anymore, assuming it would probably never happen. Baby Rosa kept them occupied and helped them keep their spirits up during their darkest hours.

It wasn't long before Antonio's assistants arrived at the bank. They sped into the car park and slammed on the breaks. The car came to a halt, and they both dived out to see a large crowd gathered in front of the bank.

They started walking more slowly, trying to look less conspicuous while finding out what was happening. As they got nearer to the bank, sirens could be heard loudly as a police van pulled up outside the bank, and a group of armed police officers surrounded the entrance.

"Please stay away!" shouted one police officer to everyone. "Do not come any closer to this building. This is a crime scene."

Clara and Jean knew that something extreme must have happened and that Antonio was involved somehow. Clara leaned towards a man in the crowd. "Please, do you know what has happened?" She prayed in her mind, that the situation was not as bad as it looked.

"The manager has shot himself," said the man.

She and Jean just stood still, trying to process this information and what it meant for them.

They held each other tightly and silently for a few minutes. They didn't know what to say. After years of making and carrying out detailed plans for this family, they were now all gone, and their minds were somewhat empty.

They walked hand-in-hand to the car and drove home, without conversation. Neither of them knew what to say, but they were unsure what would happen to Alex and Emma now.

At the bank, the police were speaking to as many staff as possible to find out what had happened and gain any inside information on what had taken place. They were told that the manager had claimed not to actually be Alex and had given details of an address where he said Alex and Emma had been hiding.

The lead police officer rounded up his team and discussed the situation for a couple of minutes. He was rapidly firing off orders about who should go where and what they should do.

After they had taken the details of every member of staff at the scene and let them go home, a group of police officers took the van to the address written on the note. Several of them had been on the team when Emma disappeared some years ago and were highly curious about this new lead they'd be given.

The investigating team of twelve people arrived at the store dressed in bulletproof vests. They pushed the door open and searched the whole place, looking through everything, but they could find absolutely nothing.

After five minutes, one of the men shouted. "Sergeant, can you come over here?" realising he'd made an interesting discovery.

The sergeant marched over, his shoes clip-clopping on the floor. "What is it?" he asked with urgency.

"We've found a door. We'll need the metal cutters, I think," he said, making sure the others were fully aware of the tough task that was likely to be at hand.

The sergeant stared at the door. "Yes, you don't see these very often any more. You four," he said, pointing to four of the biggest officers, "come here and we'll try to put it through ourselves, but I suspect we will need the metal cutters.

"Hold on, sir," said one of the officers. "Listen." They stood, hushed, and in distant tones they could make out voices and laughing.

"Right, keep calm. We need to be really careful opening this door. We don't want to hurt anyone." He shouted through the door, "Please stand clear of the door. We are not here to hurt you."

The four bulky looking officers launched themselves at the thick piece of metal, but the door was too tough for them to break down.

Two officers collected the metal cutters from the police van and meticulously cut around the door, anxious about what would be inside.

Emma and Alex were convinced their captures were coming to abuse or kill them, and they cowered in the corner, holding Rosa tightly to them and covering her eyes. "What do you want?" shouted Alex. "Why won't you leave us alone?"

"We will not hurt you. I repeat, we will not hurt you," yelled the sergeant.

The officers pushed the door through and all dropped their guns as soon as they saw the family.

The sergeant held his hands in the air to show he had no weapons. "Don't be afraid, we are the police. We won't shoot."

Emma and Alex were so jarred by their treatment that they weren't sure whether to believe these people. They stayed crouched in the corner, defenceless and terrified. Emma started to cry and held her baby tighter. They saw some light coming through the door and had mixed feelings. They were dazzled by it but at the same time apprehensive because they hadn't see even a glimpse of nature for what felt like a lifetime.

The sergeant got on his knees and looked kindly at them. He said gently, "Everything is okay. You were imprisoned here, but now you are free. You are safe."

Emma and Alex breathed out some of their nervous energy and hugged each other tightly. They had resigned themselves to the fact that they'd never be free and were struggling to take the news in, but they slowly started to believe what they were being told.

"I can see light. Oh my God, are we really free? Thank you, thank you. I don't know why we were put here, but this is incredible," said Emma, excitedly hugging one of the female police officers who had stepped nearer to her. Her eyes welled up again. She had cried so much over the years that she was surprised she had any tears left inside her. She hoped that from now on she wouldn't need to feel so extremely emotional ever again.

"Come on, come with us," said the police woman, taking her hand.

Alex was holding the baby, and they were all escorted out.

As he got nearer the outside, Alex gave the baby to Emma and ran back to write their last day on the wall. He kissed the wall. Just yesterday he wasn't sure if there would ever be a time when he would see the daylight again, and now here he was, free. He heart sang in his chest.

When they got upstairs, their eyelids crumpled, trying

to protect their eyes from this beautiful night that was now so alien to them.

They had adjusted to fake lighting for nearly four years, and it was painful to be in this atmosphere. But breathing real air and smelling London again was intense for them. They treasured each breath so deeply.

When Emma looked closely at the building, she remembered the night when she was following Rosa and when she got to the house, Antonio hit her head with the butt of his handgun. She had lost consciousness, and then when Alex arrived in the cellar, she'd blamed him, believing Antonio was Alex.

The memories sent Emma into a relapse; her mind went blind, and once more she tried to berate Alex for kidnapping her. "You son of a gun! I knew it was you, I recognised this place," she said, grabbing him and trying to attack him." The police wrenched her away and protected the baby as she lashed out.

All Emma could see was red. She was enraged with what she thought Alex had done. Alex shouted back that he didn't understand what she was mad about, and they argued violently for a minute or two.

"Stop being so angry," said Alex firmly. "You will terrify our baby."

An officer took Rosa into the police van, and the officers tried to separate the couple to stop the argument.

"Please be calm, be patient, I want to show you something," said the sergeant, trying to settle the situation. He looked at Emma and said. "Alex is right: none of this is his fault. I will show you the facts."

But Emma was acting like there was a conspiracy against her. She muttered to herself about what had happened. The officers put her in the back of the van and ignored her while they drove to the bank.

She didn't know where she was going and was confused. She needed to be sure that Alex wasn't the one that hurt her before she could trust him properly.

The van arrived at the bank, joining a bay of police vans which lined the carpark. The officers got out and then opened the doors so that Emma and Alex could get out. They were kept separate in case they tried to hurt each other again.

"I need to lie down," said Emma. "I don't want to be around all these people." She was exhausted and shell-shocked by all that was going on.

"It is important for you to understand what has happened before you can go back to any kind of normal life," said the psychologist, who had arrived to deal with any trauma that family might be suffering. She would speak to them about integrating back into the world they had involuntarily left behind.

Gradually the chattering of the staff quietened, and a chorus of gasps engulfed the carpark as it became clear to most people who was standing in front of them.

A couple of hours ago, the staff thought they'd seen Alex kill himself, and now here he was, a living, breathing man, standing plainly in front of them. And they recognised Emma, who was only a sliver of the person she used to be. Her hair was different. She was very thin, and her clothes were old, torn, and stained.

Emma and Alex looked at them, studying faces they

recognised but still overwhelmed to be in the outside world. They were speechless. Then they were both taken to see Antonio's body, lying there dishevelled and grim. It was a gruesome and tragic sight, and one which only jumbled their minds further. They both held their heads between both hands and looked at the officers questioningly.

Emma looked at the body, then looked at Alex and then looked at the body again. She kept doing this over and over, trying to fathom the strange situation. She had never met Antonio – or at least, she thought she'd never met him.

"This is Antonio, Rosa's brother. He is the one who kidnapped you both and put you in the underground," said the sergeant.

"This is unbelievable! I helped Rosa and her father Robert put Antonio in the ground years ago. I don't understand. How can this be? I was at his burial," said Alex.

Emma and Alex were taken into a private room at the bank and given some hot drinks and food and some warm, fresh clothes. Then they were shown video tapes of the recordings made at the store by Rosa, featuring Alex, so they could see what Rosa had been doing. They could see how Antonio had been preparing for his role in detail.

Alex remembered how Rosa was always recording him and keeping the recordings, and it dawned on him that his beloved was part of this crazy setup.

It took them a while to understand the true picture of what had been happening all these years, but they got there eventually and were both truly relieved that they could totally trust each other now. They gently hugged. "I'm so sorry I didn't believe you. I love you," said Emma.

Alex gave a very faint smile and put his hand through her hair. "I'm sorry too." His eyes filled with warm tears. Both felt guilty about how they'd treated each other.

The officers gave them a few moments to hold each other. After a short while, Alex turned to the policeman and asked curiously, "Where is Rosa? What happened to her?"

She frowned. "She died over a month ago, sir. I'm sorry. You will be given some counselling to cope with all the extreme pressure you are under."

Alex should not have been bothered, because Rosa had treated him so badly, living a lie with him at the centre. He should have hated her, but he didn't. She still held a special place deep in his heart and always would.

Alex and Rosa looked down at the floor, collecting their thoughts. Emma was wondering why Alex still cared for Rosa. Alex was coming to terms with the fact that he would never see Rosa alive again.

A few minutes later, a car arrived to take them to the local hospital for medical checkups. Everything was moving so quickly, but they were getting expert care, for which they were thankful.

They were given their own room with their daughter, and over the next few days the hospital examined and tested them. They spent hours with the counsellor, going through their lives, working through the situation, and trying to come to terms with things. They both felt as though heavy weights were taken off their shoulders.

But Alex's mind was still thinking of Rosa, especially

when he found out that her body was in the mortuary at the hospital. He asked the staff if he would be allowed to see her for a final time. He didn't know what he would do if he saw her, but for some reason he felt like he needed to.

His request was authorised, and he was escorted to see her that afternoon. He didn't tell Emma where he was going because he knew it would upset her; she had enough to think about.

When he arrived in the mortuary, he bowed his head and shed a tear as he looked at Rosa's porcelain face. He gazed at her for a few moments and remembered all their times together and how in love he'd been.

He leant forward and whispered, "I could never hate you, Rosa, even after all you've done. I will always love you; I can never stop." He paused and wiped his eyes with a tissue, his lip quivering.

Then with a desperate smile, holding back more tears, he said, "Do you know I am a father now? I have a daughter. Her name is Rosa. She is …" He stopped again, his throat cracking and eyes full of the tears he could no longer fight. "… beautiful, just like you. Good-bye forever, God bless your soul. I wish things could have been different."

He left her and wandered through the dowdy hospital corridors back to his family. He went over to the bed where Emma was breastfeeding Rosa. He hugged them both tightly and then lied on the bed next to them and slept for a little while, dreaming of Rosa's face. He woke in a sweat and felt very sad, but he just told Emma he couldn't remember what he'd been dreaming about. They held each other tightly, and both went to sleep with baby Rosa close by.

The next day, they were told everything was clear with their test, and they were taken from the hospital and temporarily put in a hotel to try to settle back into normal life. They would continue to have counselling in case they began to suffer from post-traumatic stress disorder.

A couple of hours later, Alex was picked up by a police escort to be taken to the bank. He would go through his old files and see what had been happening in his office since he'd been away. He wondered whether it would be possible to fit back into life in the bank, and how the staff would react to him. How much had the work changed? Would he be able to cope with new systems that would inevitably be in place by now?

The bank had been closed since the incident, although forensic tests had been finished and it would open again in a few days. It was eerily silent as he walked around, staring at the walls, the floor, and the ceiling contemplatively. It looked the same, was almost like he'd never been away.

He wondered how people's lives would have changed. Everyone apart from him and Emma had four years of life which they had lived. Alex and Emma had fallen in love and had a baby, but they had done nothing else. Would they have anything to talk to people about anymore?

He pulled open his desk and sat in his chair. The dried-up flowers the staff had bought for him were still in the middle of the desk. He read the note on the flowers and all the names that had signed it and shook his head. He wondered how they could have been so convinced that Antonio was him, but he was touched that they were so concerned.

He looked through the notes on his desk and saw that everything, from Antonio's signature to his tone of voice in writing and the way he stacked the books on his desk, was exactly the same as how he did things. It was creepy.

He scraped his chair across the floor, pushing it slightly away from the desk. He softly and bitterly laughed to himself, feeling a little stupid that Antonio had been so cunning. "I should have known how clever you are," he said out loud.

He opened each draw until he saw the book he had left before he was abducted. He pulled it out and flicked through the pages, and there it was – the note left for him by Antonio on that dark morning that he'd committed suicide.

Dear Alex,

You helped my father's plan become a reality. All my life, he'd been planning to find a lookalike for Rosa or I, so that his scheme would come to fruition. Rosa was adopted, and he only trusted me and Rosa to take care of his wealth. He encouraged us to fall in love, which we did. But all our friends would not accept us being in love, and so we had to find a double for one of us to make it acceptable.

You were my double, and for that reason alone you got caught up in this plan. It was so unfortunate for you. Emma should never have been involved, but she accidentally became part of this plan too.

You made my father very happy before he died, and you have suffered a lot of pain. Well done for getting through this, and the reward for making it through this torture is as follows:

Rosa and I are entitled to my father's inheritance, but because Rosa is also "Alex's" partner by law, and Rosa is dead, you are now entitled to Rosa's share of the inheritance. Your name is on the marriage certificate. Please be happy with the money and do good with it.

I cannot live without Rosa and I am now making a journey to her world. I hope the money will help you spend a happy life with your family.

Antonio

Alex was astounded. He couldn't believe the turn of events that had happened in his life. Not long ago he'd been wishing he was dead, but now he was thanking God that he hadn't killed himself.

He was shocked at what was happening in his life, that this grand plan dreamed up by a rich Italian merchant should end up making him rich, give him a family, give Emma her dream, and change his life so profoundly and deeply.

What a tragic twist of fate that the whole Agnoli family was dead when they had spent so many years and so much energy on delivering a plan that would never work for them – but would provide two complete strangers with a better life than they couldn't ever have imagined.

Emma had always thought she was the only one worthy of Alex, and despite everyone thinking she was deluded, this had really turned out to be the case. And now they had a beautiful child together.

Robert, Antonio, and Rosa had tried to ruin human lives for money, and in the end, the very people they tried to use and abuse to achieve their dreams were the beneficiaries.

ABOUT THE AUTHOR

Halmat S. Known by Danny D in UK.
Born in 1980 in small village called
(kallakin) few miles far from the city
of Qaladze district/Kurdistan-Iraq.